"I'M NO LONGER IN THE MARKET FOR A KNIGHT IN SHINING ARMOR, MICAH."

Surprise registered in his gray-blue eyes. "Something's happened today that's changed you. What is it?" he asked.

"I think I grew up," she confessed. "I also accepted that you weren't totally to blame for what happened two years ago with that woman. I should have been able to handle the situation better."

Micah regarded her thoughtfully for a moment, then he gently brushed his knuckles along the delicate line of her jaw. "That's more than I was expecting. I'd grown tired of the rejection I saw in your eyes every time we met."

Blythe smiled uneasily, feeling suddenly shy. "You might grow just as weary of the new me," she said quietly.

"Never, Blythe," he muttered hoarsely as he enfolded her in his arms and pulled her head against his chest. . . .

CANDLELIGHT ECSTASY SUPREMES

105 SPANISH MOON,
Beverly Wilcox Hull

106 TO LOVE A THIEF,
Joanne Bremer

107 NIGHT SHADOW,
Linda Vail

108 DANTE'S DAUGHTER,
Heather Graham

109 PERFECT CHARADE,
Alison Tyler

110 TANGLED DESTINIES,
Diana Blayne

111 WITH OPEN ARMS,
Kathy Alerding

112 PARTNERS IN PERIL,
Tate McKenna

113 NIGHT STRIKER,
Amii Lorin

114 THE WORLD IN HIS
ARMS,
JoAnna Brandon

115 RISKING IT ALL,
Caitlin Murray

116 A VERY SPECIAL
LOVER, Emily Elliott

117 DESERT PRINCESS,
Hayton Monteith

118 TREASURE FOR A
LIFETIME, Linda Vail

119 A DIFFERENT KIND OF
MAN,
Barbara Andrews

120 HIRED HUSBAND,
Melanie Catley

QUANTITY SALES

Most Dell Books are available at special quantity discounts when purchased in bulk by corporations, organizations, and special-interest groups. Custom imprinting or excerpting can also be done to fit special needs. For details write: Dell Publishing Co., Inc., 1 Dag Hammarskjold Plaza, New York, NY 10017, Attn.: Special Sales Dept., or phone: (212) 605-3319.

INDIVIDUAL SALES

Are there any Dell Books you want but cannot find in your local stores? If so, you can order them directly from us. You can get any Dell book in print. Simply include the book's title, author, and ISBN number, if you have it, along with a check or money order (no cash can be accepted) for the full retail price plus 75¢ per copy to cover shipping and handling. Mail to: Dell Readers Service, Dept. FM, P.O. Box 1000, Pine Brook, NJ 07058.

BEYOND A DOUBT

Eleanor Woods

A CANDLELIGHT ECSTASY SUPREME

Published by
Dell Publishing Co., Inc.
1 Dag Hammarskjold Plaza
New York, New York 10017

ISBN: 0-440-10655-9

Printed in the United States of America

May 1986

10 9 8 7 6 5 4 3 2 1

WFH

To Our Readers:

We are pleased and excited by your overwhelmingly positive response to our Candlelight Ecstasy Supremes. Unlike all the other series, the Supremes are filled with more passion, adventure, and intrigue, and are obviously the stories you like best.

In months to come we will continue to publish books by many of your favorite authors as well as the very finest work from new authors of romantic fiction. As always, we are striving to present unique, absorbing love stories—the very best love has to offer.

Breathtaking and unforgettable, Ecstasy Supremes follow in the great romantic tradition you've come to expect *only* from Candlelight Ecstasy.

Your suggestions and comments are always welcome. Please let us hear from you.

Sincerely,

The Editors
Candlelight Romances
1 Dag Hammarskjold Plaza
New York, New York 10017

BEYOND A
DOUBT

CHAPTER ONE

Blythe Donaldson sat at the glass-topped, white wicker table slowly sipping her first cup of coffee while she read the morning newspaper. It was early yet, not quite seven o'clock, and the sparkly dew still glistened on the spring garden beneath the bay window of the breakfast room.

As her brown eyes followed line after line of print in the article she was reading, Blythe could hear sounds from her aunts' rooms as they awakened and began their individual preparations for the day. Suddenly, two doors abruptly slammed in rapid succession. Blythe cocked her dark curly head and listened, wondering what had set off the explosion between her two elderly relatives. The muffled sound of footsteps approaching the breakfast room made her slowly shake her head. She had a pretty good idea that she was about to be drawn into the squabble.

Carrie Connors swept into the room like a grand duchess. Her rose satin robe—which Blythe knew to be at least fifteen years old—was trimmed entirely with a pale pink feather boa and appeared strangely at odds with the pink plastic curlers that were set in haphazard rows on her head.

"Good morning, Blythe dear" floated over Carrie's fragile shoulder as she glided toward the coffeepot.

"Good morning, Aunt Carrie. Are you and Aunt Amanda having a disagreement this morning?" Blythe asked innocently. It was a frequently asked question, Blythe ruefully admitted, and it was a definite advantage to be forewarned as to the topic of "discussion" between the two before she became an unwilling participant.

"My sister Amanda is getting senile," Carrie announced in her best theatrical tone, as if she were playing to one of her little-theater audiences rather than to her niece. She picked up her coffee and joined Blythe, who was always amazed that her aunt could manage to drink coffee and eat breakfast without the edges of the feathers on her sleeves getting in the way. She was truly an artist of maneuverability, Blythe decided.

"Why is Aunt Amanda becoming senile?" Blythe folded the newspaper and laid it aside, then looked inquiringly at Carrie.

"Can you believe that that twit Hamilton Davis proposed to her yesterday afternoon?"

"And?"

"She thinks it's *mahvelous*," Carrie replied in an excellent imitation of her sister.

"Didn't you go out with Mr. Davis several times, Aunt Carrie?" Blythe asked, then quickly pretended an inordinate interest in a fingernail.

A haughty sniff could be heard. "I did. But when that blond hussy moved into the apartment next to him, he became so inattentive that I dumped him."

"The women in this family do appear to have their problems with blondes, don't they? Each of Talbot's girl friends—at least the ones I knew about when we were married—were blondes."

"I really can't understand why Amanda insists on going out with him. It's an insult to

13

me," Carrie declared, not in the least swayed by Blythe's attempt to change the subject. "And to tell me that the old coot has proposed is the last straw. Can you imagine having that parasite living off us for the rest of his life?" Blythe couldn't, and she shuddered at the very thought of such a thing happening.

"I'm sure Aunt Amanda would never make the mistake of marrying Mr. Davis," Blythe said soothingly. "A proposal at her age is probably very flattering. Now that she's shared it with you, she'll forget all about it."

"What do you mean, 'her age'?" Carrie barked crossly at her niece. "She's only one year younger than I, young lady. Neither of us has been so lacking in attention from gentlemen callers that we have to rejoice when the likes of Hamilton Davis proposes. Should have taken a whip to him."

"To Mr. Davis?" Blythe asked in surprise.

"No. To Talbot. I do think the eyes on that ex-husband of yours are built on swivels so he can watch ten different females at the same time. You should have married Micah." She sat back, a pleasant smile wreathing her face, momentarily forgetting Mr. Davis and Amanda. "Now that was a man for you."

"Oh, I agree, Auntie, he was and, I suppose,

still is quite a man. But I could never quite get used to those strange women I found in his bed," Blythe murmured. She was sitting forward in her chair by this time, with one elbow on the table and her chin resting on the heel of her palm, staring into space. "Trying to pass them off as Stephen's friends was a bit much."

"Perhaps they were Stephen's. His brother was around a lot that summer. Somehow Micah never struck me as a liar."

"You've always believed his story, haven't you?" Blythe stared thoughtfully at Carrie.

"He was such a devil," Carrie said simply, "and he was always so nice to Amanda and me. There was no pretense about him. He reminded me of some wild, spirited stallion roaming the plains. My only fault with Micah was that he hurt you. I find that difficult to forgive."

"Talbot was and is equally as nice to you and Aunt Amanda as Micah." Blythe felt compelled to defend her former husband, though she was at a loss to understand why. Unless, she mused, it had simply become a habit during her short marriage to convince herself and her aunts that Talbot was just as much a man as Micah Caine. It had taken her only three or four weeks to realize that she'd married on the rebound. But even with that uncomfortable thought always in the back of her mind, she'd done everything possible to make the marriage work.

"You're right, of course. And I still like Talbot. Otherwise, I wouldn't have let him continue to handle my investments. As husbands go, though, I don't rate him very high on my list."

"You don't rate any man very high on your list, sister dear," Amanda Benson said bluntly as she entered the breakfast room, her snow-white hair piled attractively atop her head. She walked over and dropped a kiss on Blythe's forehead, bringing the fresh scent of lavender with her, then continued on to the coffeepot. "The only men you tolerate are the ones you can manipulate. Otherwise, you have no use for them." She walked over and plunked down a cup of hot coffee, then sat and glared at her sister. "I just might marry Hamilton Davis. What do you think of that?"

"I think it would be terrible, and I would disinherit you," Carrie threatened.

"Don't be ridiculous," Amanda scoffed. "Leave everything to Blythe. I have more money than you do anyway. The least we can do for our niece is to leave her with enough money so she won't be forced to marry for security."

"That is the silliest damn thing I've ever heard," Carrie declared, glaring. "Women don't marry for security these days. Why, they go out into the world and compete with the men. Marriage is a fifty-fifty deal."

"That's why the divorce rate is so high," Amanda said, disgusted. She looked at Blythe. "She makes marriage sound like a business deal between two people. I may be old-fashioned, but when a woman needs that little extra attention from her husband, she doesn't expect to have to write a memo or go through a board meeting to get it. No," she said resolutely, "there are some things that just don't change. Why, I never even considered burning *my* bra."

Blythe looked to Carrie for a reply and wasn't disappointed. The conversation continued, hot and furious. Blythe's head went back and forth as she followed the action. As she listened, it struck her again how very much the two arguing women meant to her. They were her family. They and Greenleigh, their home—it had been built before the Civil War—where they all now lived, was all that

17

remained of the Donaldsons. Her father had been their baby brother. He and Blythe's mother had died in a plane crash, leaving eight-year-old Blythe in the care of Carrie and Amanda. A smile of gentle forbearance pulled at her lips as she remembered the transition from her first home, where the love between her parents had created such a tranquil setting, to the mule-and-donkey atmosphere in which her aunts existed at Greenleigh.

And yet, Blythe thought as she turned a deaf ear to the argument regarding the disposition of Carrie's money, Mr. Davis' attentions, and the burning of Amanda's bra, she'd found the sudden change in her young life exciting. The South, especially Mobile and its sunny summers, had seemed like heaven to the young girl used to the frigid harshness of Maine winters. Her parents, although they had been very kind, had been too wrapped up in their love for each other to pay much attention to their daughter. Not so with her aunts; Blythe became the center of their somewhat unusual lives. And as is the nature of all things, she thought a little sadly, over the years their roles had slowly reversed, and now she was the mainstay in their lives.

"Ladies, I do hate to break up this happy threesome." She smiled at Carrie and Amanda. "But I have to dress and get to the shop. Any errands for me today?"

"I haven't gotten my monthly statement from Talbot," Carrie said. "Do you suppose you could stop by and get it for me? I could go into town today, but I have quite a bit of correspondence to catch up on."

"Don't be ridiculous, Carrie," her sister admonished. "Talbot Ames is Blythe's ex-husband, for Pete's sake! She doesn't want to be constantly popping in and out of his office like a yo-yo. Call him on the phone and tell him to get off his behind and send you what you want. You could also use a *real* broker and save yourself a lot of headaches."

Carrie adopted a thoroughly injured expression, sticking her nose so high in the air that it was all Blythe could do to keep from laughing. As for stopping by Talbot's office, she hoped that had been settled. Carrie had left her stock portfolio with Talbot even after he and Blythe were divorced. Under normal circumstances Blythe would have objected. But her aunt was getting on in years and viewed any drastic change in her business affairs as inviting certain doom. Consequently,

Blythe had found herself having to do some fancy maneuvering in order to avoid becoming a handy messenger between the two. Although it was true she and Talbot weren't exactly enemies, she hadn't the slightest desire to cultivate a more than casual relationship with her ex-husband.

Blythe pushed her chair back and rose to her feet. Before leaving the room, she dropped a kiss on the cheek of each aunt. "I have a small shipment of handbags coming in today, Aunt Amanda. I ordered two for you that I think you'll like. There's also a robe that came in yesterday, Aunt Carrie, that would look like a dream on you. See you this evening."

As she left the battlefront quickly and headed for her room, she couldn't help but chuckle. She'd learned long ago that either aunt could and would get her feelings hurt if Blythe failed to remember them equally.

Having her own dress shop was a luxury when it came to clothes, Blythe decided pleasantly after putting on her makeup and her beige lingerie. She ran a quick hand over a pale apricot two-piece linen suit lined with a silky cream material, enjoying the feel of the crisp fabric beneath her fingertips. She slipped on a blouse and the suit, and stepped into beige pumps that added at least two inches to her five-foot-two height, then walked over to the rosewood dresser and opened her jewelry box.

As she poked among the various pieces of jewelry that she'd accumulated over the years, in search of something to wear with the suit, her gaze fell on a tiny black velvet box tucked in one corner. It had been months since she'd opened that box, but for some reason that she couldn't explain, her hand now went unerringly to it and picked it up. As though expecting a genie to leap from the velvet confines and cast a spell over her, she gently eased up the lid and stared at the perfect cut and clarity of the large diamond solitaire. It was the engagement ring Micah Caine had given her.

She moved the ring slightly, watching the way the morning sun caught and reflected the different facets of the stone. Blythe often wondered why she had kept the ring. Was there some masochistic streak in her? Was it a reminder of the man who had betrayed her, kept so that she would never make the same mistake again? Or was she simply unable to bring herself to dispose of that last tangible link that she had thought would bind Micah to her forever?

The abrupt closing of the tiny box in her hand sounded loud in the stillness of the bedroom. Blythe shook her head quickly in an effort to wipe away memories that refused to die. She put the ring back in her jewelry box, telling herself that a stone of its size and value should be in the safe deposit box at the bank, but she somehow never seemed able to get it there. The ring, like her thoughts of Micah, seemed destined to remain with her.

As she tried once again to decide which necklace would look best with the suit she was wearing, Blythe couldn't help but remember the agony of the sleepless night she'd endured after finding Micah in another woman's arms, and of the following morning, when she'd determined to give back the ring. Micah had betrayed her, and she'd wanted nothing from him.

Carrie and Amanda had been appalled when they learned she was planning on sending the ring by messenger to the Gulf Shore condominium complex where Micah was staying, which he was thinking of adding to his own chain of hotels. Too weary to argue, Blythe gave in to her aunts' antiquated idea that such an undertaking should be conducted by family, not by some cold, impersonal stranger. Two hours later, they were back, looking faintly harassed, with the ring and an announcement from Micah that as far as he was concerned, he and Blythe were still engaged.

Three months later, quite evidently on the rebound, Blythe had married Talbot Ames. Approximately four months later, they had separated; their divorce was final the following month.

Now, two years later, after her marriage to Talbot and her subsequent divorce from him, there could be little doubt in Micah Caine's mind that the engagement was well and truly off, Blythe thought maliciously as she looked at her reflection in the dresser mirror. Don't do this, she warned herself. Don't allow Micah to creep into your thoughts and ruin a perfectly beautiful day.

But the thoughts were there. Blythe shrugged in defeat; there was very little she could do about them. She picked up her purse and left her bedroom, anxious to get to work.

"Where do you want to display these swimsuits, Blythe?" Ainsley Stone asked.

Ainsley was an artist; her gallery-studio was located at the same address as Blythe's Boutique. Throwing up a partition and making room for the studio had worked well for both, giving Blythe some relief from the high rent she was paying, and enabling Ainsley an affordable and choice location.

"Hmmm," Blythe murmured thoughtfully as her eyes darted over the two remaining spaces closest to the entrance. "I suppose one of those circular racks nearest the door would be best." She quickly put the armful of blouses she was holding on a chair and hurried to the front of the shop. "Give me a sec to move these slacks over there," she said, nodding toward the companion rack on the other side of the aisle.

After rehanging the slacks and displaying the swimsuits, Blythe turned to Ainsley. "How about a cup of coffee?"

"Please. I came to work around six this morning, and I'm still half asleep." The tall, slim redhead yawned as she followed Blythe to the stockroom.

"Sounds like business is good," Blythe remarked. She poured coffee into two mugs, handed one to Ainsley, then sat on the edge of a long worktable from where she could see the front door.

"It is. I've sold two of my landscapes this week, plus Jim's atrocity."

"I don't believe it." Blythe shuddered. "Who on earth would want that awful thing?"

"A charming little old lady who looks like everybody's idea of their aunt—excluding your aunts, of course." Ainsley chuckled. "She thought it would be perfect for 'her husband's haunt.' "

"What is her husband's haunt like, a house of horrors?"

"I don't quiz my patrons, dear. If they want something, I sell it. I'm totally mercenary. Oh, before I forget, what are your plans for the weekend?"

"I'm flexible. Anything particular in mind?"

"Sean is having a few people down to the beach house Saturday night. We could leave as soon as we close and come back early Monday morning."

"Couples?"

"Not necessarily. You know how Sean's parties usually go. People come and go. Very relaxed."

"I'll think about it," Blythe promised. "But

since I don't have a date, I'd probably feel out of place."

"I doubt it." Ainsley grinned. "The comers and goers at Sean's affairs usually mean two men for every woman. You might meet someone interesting."

"I'll think about," Blythe repeated.

"How did you leave the terrible twins this morning?" Coming from a cool and distant family environment, Ainsley found her friend's aunts a constant source of amusement, yet at the same time she envied them their closeness.

"Arguing. Aunt Amanda is seeing one of Aunt Carrie's former friends. He proposed to Amanda, and Carrie was ready to have said former friend shot."

"Did you tell Amanda that you had a handbag for her that would hold at least a week's supply of groceries?"

"Right after she got through giving Aunt Carrie a stern lecture for asking me to stop by Talbot's office sometime during the day."

"Your family is weird," Ainsley drawled, "but nice. I'd think your ex-husband would be the one Carrie would want to shoot, after the way he treated you."

"I suppose she would, if I'd been really

hurt," Blythe said thoughtfully. "But for the life of me, after I got over the initial shock, I realized that I just didn't care how many mistresses Talbot had."

Just then the buzzer connected to the front door sounded in the stockroom. Ainsley rose from the straight chair and stretched. "Want me to go out front while you count those?" she asked, indicating the necklaces, bracelets, and other accessories that Blythe was checking against the invoice sheet.

"Please."

Several minutes passed as Blythe worked her way through the merchandise. Occasionally the sound of voices from the front penetrated her thoughts, but for the most part she ignored everything but the paperwork at hand.

As she was bending over to reach one last bundle of belts, she felt a large, warm hand skim lightly over her back and settle on the slight swell of her buttocks. Ordinarily such a thing would have sent Blythe up and around with her arm swinging, but in this case she didn't do that. Instead, she managed to get her fingers on the belts and then straightened, her back turned, her face expressionless as she counted each item and then marked it off on the invoice.

"I'm disappointed in your technique, Micah," she finally said coolly. "A mere hello would have been sufficient."

CHAPTER TWO

As she turned around, Blythe felt her body unconsciously bracing itself for that first look into his staggering gray-blue eyes. In fact, she put off that particular moment and let her gaze skim along the incredible length of him, finally move to the rough-hewn cragginess of his face.

There'd been no change there in the three months since she'd last seen him, but change wasn't exactly what Blythe was looking for, or so she kept telling herself. Each time she saw him, she hoped that her heart would cease hammering like crazy and that her breath wouldn't rush in and out of her lungs.

"What brings you to Mobile?" she finally

asked, trying to still the dizziness that threatened to overwhelm her, and finding the angle of his jaw and stubborn chin still as fascinating as ever. She was sure he'd given up the condominium at Gulf Shore—hadn't he? Blythe searched frantically through the back of her mind, trying to remember if there had been any sort of pattern to the different times he'd casually dropped by the boutique—just to irritate her? Knowing that he kept mainly to the eastern coast of Florida made him far easier to deal with.

"I have an appointment at ten-thirty," he drawled huskily, the tone of his voice as caressing as ever. "After that, I thought maybe you'd have lunch with me." As he spoke, Micah was silently damning Stephen to hell. If it hadn't been for his brother's desire to see how many women he could entice into his bed, Micah and Blythe would have been married now, and there'd be no reason for him to be standing here like this, aching to have her in his arms.

"I'm afraid I already have plans for lunch," Blythe said quietly as her gaze lingered on the dark-blond crispness of his hair. She didn't need to touch it to reacquaint herself with its texture. Her fingertips were already tingling with the memory. She'd often teased him about having it trimmed so that it wouldn't curl. She remembered other things about him as well, including the tiny half-moon birthmark on his right thigh and the way she'd caressed that spot with her fingers and her lips.

"What are they?"

"What?" Blythe looked confused. She took a step backward, determined to break the unbelievable electricity arching between them.

"Your plans," Micah gruffly reminded her, seeing the same longing in her eyes that had haunted him for so long.

"Oh. I have to see Talbot." She said the first thing that popped into her mind.

Micah felt the beginnings of deep rage stirring within him at the mention of Talbot Ames. "I wasn't aware that you and your ex-husband were still on friendly terms. I thought any man who was unfaithful to you was automatically banished from your sight forever."

"Is there any reason why we should be enemies just because we couldn't live together?" she asked defiantly.

"He was unfaithful to you, wasn't he?" Micah bluntly reminded her. He leaned against the edge of the table and crossed his arms over his chest, obviously in no hurry to leave.

"Do you keep track of the causes of all the divorce in this area?"

"No. Only the one that pleased me."

"That's a horrible thing to admit. I wanted my marriage with Talbot to work."

"That's bull, Blythe darling, and you know it," Micah was quick to point out. "You married that slick-tongued bastard on the rebound from me. I wonder when you'll be woman enough to face up to it?"

"I'm woman enough to face up to a number of things, Micah." She smiled coolly. "Don't you remember? I faced up rather quickly to the fact that you had a revolving door in your condo. When I wasn't around, you entertained all sorts of interesting people. I especially remember a redhead and a blonde as being among them."

Micah reached for her then, a wave of shimmery anger washing before his eyes. "Damn you," he cried hoarsely as his large hands caught hold of her shoulders and shook her. "I told you—those women were nothing to me. I barely knew them. Stephen had just gotten out of the marines and wanted to celebrate.

From the way he was going about it, I think he probably tried to sleep with every woman within a fifty-mile radius that week."

The dizziness she'd felt earlier was nothing compared with the combination of the shaking and the touch of his hands. Blythe could feel the depth of his warmth seeping throughout her body. Suddenly, she twisted out of his hands, knowing that if she didn't, the next thing she knew she would be in his arms. "I know. You told me a number of times what happened after I tried to return your ring. Well, I grew tired of hearing that story, Micah," she said shakily. "I also grew tired of trying to figure out why I found you in your private suite, almost naked, kissing 'Stephen's blonde.' Were you trying to get to know her better, or were you just being brotherly and helping him keep his stable of women happy?" *Damn him!* Blythe thought. She didn't want to rehash all the unhappiness he'd caused her. Just seeing him was bad enough. But for him to stand before her and continue to try to get her to believe such a ridiculous tale was too much.

"I can't see how it's humanly possible for a woman of your supposed intelligence to still believe that I was unfaithful to you."

"It had something to do with the passive way you 'accepted' the blonde's advances," Blythe retorted. "When I noticed the towel around your hips beginning to slip, I knew you weren't going to put up much of a fight. Care to elaborate?"

"Elaborate, hell!" Micah yelled, his face growing uncomfortably red. "I'd like to box your ears, you stubborn little witch."

"Oh, really?" Blythe yelled back, her chest rising and falling rapidly. "Well, let me be the first to tell you, Mr. Caine, that *I* wasn't the one caught in a compromising situation. I'd heard all sorts of wild tales about you, but I was fool enough to think I was the one to tame you." A low, mirthless sound resembling a laugh escaped her. "What a fool I was."

"You *were* the one that tamed me." Micah took a step toward her, then stopped. "On the other hand, since you've proved to be so damn stupid, I'm beginning to think I'm lucky."

"Stupid!" Blythe cried incredulously. "How dare you stand there and call me stupid?" She threw the now-crumpled invoice to the floor and flung out her arm imperiously, her forefinger pointing toward the door. "Get out of my shop this instant," she ordered. "And another thing. I will be returning your ring—again—and this time you'd better accept it."

"And if I don't?"

"Then I'll sell it and send the money to a home for retired hookers—I'm sure you'll have any number of acquaintances there," she cried sarcastically.

"I'm sure they'd appreciate the gesture," he infuriated her by saying. "But before I go, there's one thing I'd like to know."

"What's that?" Blythe asked suspiciously.

"This," Micah smoothly answered and reached for her again. Before Blythe could step out of his reach, he'd pulled her against his chest, his arms like bands of steel encircling her and keeping her prisoner. His head dipped and his mouth crushed hers as his tongue forced its way between her lips and ran along the surface of her teeth. "Open your mouth, Blythe," he whispered, "or we can play this little game all day."

Whether it was his threat or the curious rush of longing flooding over her, Blythe wasn't certain. She opened to him, though, the tip of her tongue welcoming his bold demanding kiss. Her body, stiff and unyielding at first, slowly became pliant and soft, curving against his hard thighs and broad chest. Her hands went unerringly to the rough texture of his hair, which had always so intrigued her; her fingertips ruffled through the thickness, then quietly molded themselves to the shape of his head.

Micah could feel the blood thundering through his veins as he felt her firm round breasts flattened against his chest, breasts he'd seen and touched and kissed so many times. His breathing became harsh and labored as his hands ran possessively over Blythe's back, settling on her buttocks and pressing her against him. Regardless of what she said, he told himself, he could feel the fire in her, could sense the passion and desire running through her slender body. *God!* he all but groaned, she was still in his blood, still capable of making him forget everything but what it was like making love to her. He wanted her, and he would have her, he promised himself as he lifted his head and inhaled deeply, the scent of her filling his nostrils and making him dizzy with desire.

With a determination that was directly at odds with what he was feeling, he eased Blythe back, his hands firm on her upper arms. A gleam of triumph was reflected in his blue-gray eyes as he closely scrutinized her flushed face. "For a woman who would have me believe she hates my guts, I find your response to my kiss somewhat of a surprise."

Blythe ran her fingertips over her swollen lips and dropped her gaze. Conversation with Micah at this point was something she absolutely refused to get involved in. "Please go, Micah," she whispered.

His large hand snaked out, the palm fitting itself to the curve of her hot cheek, his thumb lightly caressing her lips. "Don't take it so hard, princess," he murmured. "I've experienced those same gut-wrenching thoughts you're having at the moment."

"You have no idea what my thoughts are," Blythe said softly. She turned to the table where the merchandise she'd been checking was still waiting. She gripped the edge with both hands, knowing that if she tried to pick up something, her hands would tremble so badly she would drop it.

"Oh yes, Blythe darling, I do." She saw him lean forward, both his hands splayed close beside hers on the tabletop. "I know that you still want me just as much as I want you, but you're too stubborn to admit it. If I wanted to, I could take you to bed this very moment and have you begging me to make love to you."

"If you're so positive of your power over me, then why don't you do it?" Blythe challenged, her voice still wobbly. But even as she spoke the words, she prayed he wouldn't try. If he did, she was terribly afraid he would succeed.

"Because I have too much pride to force you," he surprised her by saying. "I want you to come to me on your own—just as you left me."

"I can never do that. I also have my pride—which you walked all over more than two years ago."

"And you sought revenge against me by marrying Talbot Ames, right?"

"I loved Talbot," Blythe replied spiritedly, her head high.

"That's a damn lie!"

"Think what you will." She shrugged, and a meager normalcy returned to her emotions and her body now that she was out of his arms. "What we had is dead, Micah. I've put it out of my mind."

"It's not over for either of us, and you know it. It'll never be over, and I have no intention of letting you stick your head in the sand to avoid it." He swung around to leave, but after taking only a couple of steps he turned and looked at Blythe. "I think it's only fair to warn you that since you aren't willing to be honest with me, we'll just have to play out this little charade by *my* rules."

Blythe retrieved the mangled invoice and picked up her pen. "The charade you speak of is in your head, Micah. My plans for the future do not include you."

"I *am* your future, Blythe. You'd be well advised to remember that. By the way, do whatever you want with the ring—I think I'll buy you another one. That one reminds me too much of Ames."

Before Blythe could tell him what he could do with both his rings, he was gone, his long stride carrying him effortlessly through the shop and out the front door.

She leaned weakly against the edge of the table, willing the world around her to stop spinning.

"Wow!" A big-eyed Ainsley exclaimed as she zipped through the doorway into the stockroom. "That was some confrontation the two of you had. I'm sorry to say it, but I listened to every word. It was wonderful."

"Well, I'm glad someone enjoyed it, because I didn't," Blythe said haughtily. *Yes she did*, her conscience jeered. She enjoyed every single, heartbreaking minute of it. The only trouble was, she was too stubborn to admit it. "Micah is a closed book in my life."

"Ha!" Ainsley snorted knowingly. "And pigs can fly, right? Oh well," she mused thoughtfully, her gaze lingering on the front door, through which Micah had stormed. "It will be interesting to see how all this will work out."

" 'All this' isn't going to work out," Blythe snapped. "Micah Caine is no longer a part of my life. Why is it so difficult to get that point across?"

"Several reasons, none of which I care to go into at the moment." Ainsley suddenly became the epitome of diplomacy. "I don't care to be evicted, nor do I want my rent raised. Either would probably happen if I pursued this conversation."

"I couldn't have put it better myself," Blythe said as the front buzzer sounded again. "If you'll excuse me, Ms. Stone," she murmured, then walked calmly from the room, her head held high.

Blythe glanced down at her watch for the third or fourth time in less than fifteen minutes and then back at the tall, bearded man in scruffy jeans and faded blue shirt who was positioning several nice landscapes about the gallery. At least, Blythe thought they were nice. She certainly wasn't in Ainsley's knowledgeable class when it came to art, but the paintings were by far the best she'd seen up to this point in the gallery.

Blythe also decided that if Ainsley and all her arty wisdom didn't hurry up and get back from lunch and deal with the stern-featured individual who she assumed was the artist, she was going to clobber her. Blythe was still a little disconcerted at finding the man in the shop in the first place, calmly making himself at home without a word to anyone.

She walked over to where the first two paintings were now hanging, and she stared at them. Even to an untrained eye it was evident that they were far superior to any of the others that Ainsley had taken on consignment.

"I'm sorry Ainsley is late getting back from lunch—she's usually very prompt. She must have gotten your appointment confused with another." Blythe turned and was surprised to find the man standing quite close, openly staring at her.

"I doubt that."

"Oh, I assure you, Ainsley is very reliable," Blythe was quick to inform him. Really, she was thinking as she was speaking, the man is almost hostile. His abrupt manner and the fact that he hadn't once smiled since she had discovered his presence were beginning to make her nervous. And he certainly wasn't the sharpest dresser either, she reasoned, but then immediately discarded that notion. A number of the artists who did business with Ainsley had been similarily attired.

"I'm sure she is." Mr. Congeniality unbent enough to nod his dark head the briefest fraction in agreement. "Do you work for Ms.— er—"

"Stone," Blythe supplied, "Ainsley Stone. No, I don't work for her. I own the boutique next door. We're close friends." Good grief, she thought, he doesn't even know Ainsley. But he'd appeared so at home. Blythe fidgeted nervously, not knowing whether to ask him to take his paintings and leave or to lock the door and not let him escape. "It's such an unusual name, I'm surprised you forgot it."

"There's no reason why I should remember your friend's name," the man curtly remarked. "I've never met her."

"But you—I mean—" Blythe at first

floundered, then became annoyed. "Don't you think it would have been thoughtful of you to have told me this in the beginning?"

"Now, why should I have done that?" he had the gall to ask. "Your friend has a small but nice place to display works of art. I'm an artist." He shrugged. "What's the big fuss about?"

"Because, Mr.—whoever you are—it would have been the considerate thing to do," Blythe bluntly informed him. "I have a business to run, and I don't have time to stand watch over every shifty-eyed character who wanders in off the street. That's what the big fuss is about. There's also the fact that Ainsley just might not want to display your paintings." She threw that in for the heck of it, though in her heart she felt that Ainsley would be crazy not to take them.

A curious grin of appreciation slowly crept into the man's dark eyes as he watched Blythe. He leaned his hips against one of several sturdy tables in the shop, his hands thrust into the back pockets of his jeans. "Has anyone ever told you that you're a very beautiful woman?"

"Yes," Blythe said calmly. Inwardly she was wondering how in the world she'd gotten into such a mess. "What does that have to do with you pushing your way in here without an appointment, Mr.—?"

"Derek Hampton. Your name?"

"Blythe Donaldson."

"Married?"

"I beg your pardon?" Blythe stared at him.

"Are you married? You aren't wearing a ring, but these days one can't go by that."

"No," Blythe shook her head, "I'm not married." She began to edge her way behind the sturdy counter.

"Neither am I."

"Well, I'm sure you must be very happy with that arrangement," she answered for lack of a better reply, though privately she was wondering who in her right mind would ever want to marry such a scowling devil. "Er, if you have something else to do, I'll be happy to take down any information you care to give me and pass it on to Ainsley."

"I'm in no hurry," he said pleasantly, then took a couple of steps forward and leaned against the counter. "I'd much rather spend my time talking with you. Now that we've introduced ourselves, would you have dinner with me this evening?"

"No. I have other plans." The man was a

nut, she told herself as she nervously waited for him to leave or for Ainsley to return.

"Tomorrow evening?" he persisted.

"Mr. Hampton, it's barely been fifteen minutes since we met," Blythe pointed out to him. Her patience with this guy was beginning to run thin. "I don't care to go out with strangers."

"Pity." He shrugged laconically. "Perhaps you'll let me paint you—once you get to know me better."

Blythe was on the point of telling him that she had no desire to be painted by him or anyone else when the door opened and Ainsley came bustling in, followed by Micah. It couldn't be, Blythe told herself as she watched their approach, it simply couldn't be. One visit from Micah had gotten her day off to a lousy start; two would destroy it altogether.

"I'm sorry to have been so long," Ainsley murmured as she zipped behind the counter and stashed her purse in a drawer. "I only just met Micah at the door." She looked at Derek Hampton, who hadn't bothered moving from his position, and then back at Blythe.

"This is Mr. Hampton, Ainsley," Blythe informed her friend with a sugary smile. "He's brought in several paintings, which he's already hung."

"I'll give you a ring tomorrow in case you change your mind about dinner with me," Derek said smoothly.

"Don't bother," Micah neatly nixed the idea in a commanding voice. "She's having dinner with me." He caught Blythe by the arm and hustled her from the gallery, his craggy features set in a deep scowl.

"What the hell was that all about?" he demanded the moment they were in the boutique.

"A dinner invitation that I had already refused," Blythe told him. She walked over and began straightening several dresses on the wall rack. "I appreciate your stepping in when you did; he doesn't seem to be a man who takes no for an answer."

"Perhaps I should have a talk with him." Even without looking at him, Blythe knew his jaw was set determinedly and that there was a menacing glare in his eyes.

She smiled in spite of her resolve to keep him at a safe distance. "I think you got your point across." She felt rather than heard Micah walk over to stand directly behind her;

the heat from his body reached out and caressed her with its intensity.

"Go out with me this evening," he said softly. Though he made no effort to touch her, his nearness was enough to send sharp fissures of awareness skimming along the surface of her skin.

"I'm busy."

"Liar," he whispered mockingly. "You're afraid, aren't you?"

"Not afraid, just cautious," Blythe murmured as she stared blindly at the colorful array of dresses in front of her.

"I think you're a coward. Prove me wrong by going out with me."

"No."

"Do you really think I'm going to give up so easily?"

"I really haven't thought about it," Blythe confessed. She turned and faced him. Their bodies were so close that the tips of her breasts brushed the dark fabric of his suit jacket. "Why have you suddenly decided to camp on my doorstep?" she demanded, taking a step back.

"Because I found myself growing weary of this cat-and-mouse game you've been playing." He moved closer, forcing Blythe to either stand her ground or become smothered in the season's latest fashions. "We've met several times at different events since your divorce. I've also dropped by here on occasion, as well as called you a number of times. Each time we've met, you've acted like I was a leper."

"All of which should prove to you that I don't want to pick up our relationship as though nothing happened." Her palms were moist with perspiration and she was finding it very difficult to pull her gaze away from the sensuous invitation of his lips.

"But I want to resume that relationship, princess." Micah's hand stole ever so slowly over her shoulder and dipped lower, the tips of his fingers brushing intimately—deliberately—against the firmness of one breast. "I want you back. Back in my arms so I can make love to you till you cry out for mercy. I want you with me always."

"And my wants?" she somehow managed to ask.

"Are the same as mine." He smiled, although it was far from happy. "You tried to escape me by running off and marrying Ames. You should have learned something from that bitter experience."

"The marriage wasn't all that bad," Blythe said in defense, though she knew it was a futile gesture.

"It was bad enough to send your husband of a few months looking for a warmer bed, sweetheart," Micah said bluntly, his eyes unashamedly devouring each of her features. *You couldn't keep him or any other man satisfied, because you belong to me. It's like that with some people. Once you accept that, we can get on with our lives."

"I'll fight you to hell and back before I allow you to wreck my life again, Micah." The words were softly spoken, but the thread of determination could be heard in them as well.

"Then my advice to you, Blythe Donaldson, is to keep your guard up at all times. I had you once, and I'll damn sure have you again. But this time there'll be no reason for you to run. I'll make doubly certain of that."

CHAPTER THREE

By the end of the day, Blythe felt drained. Micah's two visits had left her with a sense of disenchantment, as if the life she'd worked so hard to make for herself were lacking in some way. But it was only a temporary feeling, she reasoned as she called her part-time help for the next day and closed up the shop; it had to be. She was convinced that she'd made the right decision where Micah was concerned.

On her way home, Blythe's mind slipped back to when she'd met Micah. It had been during the holiday season. She'd gone to a Christmas party with Bill Comer, a man she dated from time to time. The mood that evening had been festive and carefree. But

Blythe felt poleaxed when Micah Caine stepped in front of her, removed the glass from her fingers, and led her to the dance floor. In later, desperate moments of introspection, she blamed the wine she had consumed, declaring it must have gone straight to her brain.

In his arms she'd promptly forgotten Bill, forgotten that she was one of a close circle of friends that partied together and usually rounded out the evening—or early morning —by having breakfast together before going their separate ways. She'd become lost in a pair of gray-blue eyes that had cast a spell over her as surely as if some magic potion had been mysteriously added to one of her glasses of wine.

Remembering that evening still bewildered Blythe as she probed the inexplicable web that Micah had woven around her. His power and strength had permeated her senses as he kept her by his side or in his arms for the remainder of the evening and then took her home. His good-night kiss had left her reeling in the aftermath of emotions that had at first frightened her and then slowly became capsulized into a shimmering, glowing intensity that shone from her eyes and turned her days and nights into an unbeliev-able paradise. Micah became the king in that paradise and she his willing slave.

Blythe fidgeted nervously as she waited for a traffic light to change to green. She closed her eyes for a brief second in a futile attempt to expunge from her mind the months follow-ing the party, but she was finding—as had happened so often in the past—that where Micah Caine was concerned, she was still a slave to him somewhat, if only in her thoughts.

By the time she reached the tree-lined drive that led to Greenleigh, Blythe had man-aged—through sheer forcefulness—to con-centrate on the last-minute details she had to take care of in the morning for the sale that started the next day at the boutique. She stopped at the mailbox at one side of the drive, reached inside, and removed the mail. Thumbing through it, she couldn't help but grin. The aunts would be in seventh heaven. There were a number of letters for them that Blythe recognized as information on or notifi-cation of them being winners in contests. Amanda and Carrie had been bitten by the contest bug for as long as Blythe could re-member. She shook her head in amusement as she traveled the short distance to the Creole-style home that had been built in the early eighteen-hundreds and to the garage at the rear. When she'd first arrived at Greenleigh, she'd joined her relatives in their favorite pastime. But as she'd grown up, her interest in contests had waned. For the last six or seven years, due to the fact that Amanda and Carrie had become experts at winning, it had become Blythe's job to dispose of many of the prizes they received. A number of the charitable organizations in town went into a quiet panic when they saw her pulling up in the ancient station wagon that refused to die.

Having always been of a philanthropic nature, Carrie and Amanda were quick to share their winnings with others less fortunate. Thus, Blythe's arrival from time to time at various places with such items as fifty safari hats, a moose head measuring five feet from antler tip to antler tip, or ten cases of Dry Gulch Willie's hot chili, could cause people to blanch visibly. The list was endless and most times the items ranged from the ridiculous to the exotic.

Blythe smiled with characteristic good humor as she parked the car and gathered up the mail, her purse, and a large light-blue paper bag with the name of her boutique written across it. The reception their gifts received—whether good or bad—failed to deter her aunts. They forged ahead like two tiny generals, gathering in their contest prizes and generously dispensing them.

The moment she entered the back door, Blythe detected the tempting aroma of seafood gumbo. She went through the old butler's pantry into the kitchen, where she found both her aunts swathed in aprons from hemline to chin and bustling about, brandishing spoons like tiny swords.

"Hello," she called out cheerfully.

"Blythe dear." Amanda looked around and smiled. She immediately dipped a spoon into the pot, then hurried over to her niece. "You must taste this gumbo. Carrie says it needs more pepper, but I think a touch more garlic would do the trick."

Blythe placed the things she was carrying on the table, then opened her mouth and tasted. "Mmm." She closed her eyes appreciatively. "I think it's just right." She knew from experience that if she'd favored either suggestion it would have meant instant war.

"Do you really think so, dear?" Carrie

asked. She'd walked over as well and had been waiting anxiously for the decision.

"Perfect." Blythe smiled as she stepped closer and dropped a kiss on each waiting cheek. "How much longer does it have to simmer?" she asked hopefully.

"At least another hour," Amanda replied, checking the clock on the stove.

"Well, that'll give me time to grab a quick shower and let the two of you look over what I brought you, won't it?" Blythe turned back to the table and reached inside the bag. "This is for you, Aunt Carrie." She handed her aunt a lovely lilac satin robe, trimmed with white fur. "And this is for you, Aunt Amanda." The bag was almost as large as her aunt, whose face broke into a huge smile.

"It's perfect! Now I can put all my important things in here and not have to worry about not having enough room."

"When did that ever stop you before?" Carrie piped up. "You look like a bag woman now, with all those huge purses you cart around."

"Well, at least I don't look like a floozie, floating around in those damn feathers," Amanda shot back without hesitation.

"Must you be so coarse?" Carrie sniffed, her chin so high it almost blocked her vision.

"I only express myself in the privacy of my family. Besides, it's good for the system."

"Girls, girls," Blythe stepped between them, slipping an arm around each one. "Let's not argue. You each have different and distinct tastes, and I love you both just the way you are."

"Your aunt gives me a pain in the—"

"Aunt Amanda," Blythe quickly interrupted, "let's call a truce. Tell me who's coming to dinner. You only cook gumbo for very special people. Who is it this time?"

Suddenly, it was as if both women had lost their ability to speak. They leaned forward simultaneously and peered at each other. Blythe frowned as she watched them. Could they possibly have reached an agreement regarding Mr. Davis? She certainly hoped so; it would make life much more agreeable for all concerned if that had happened.

"Er—why don't you go on and have your shower, dear?" Amanda suggested. She paused for a moment as if she wanted to say something, then thought better of it and walked over to the stove.

Carrie threw her niece a guarded glance and followed her sister.

"Okay." Blythe crossed her arms over her

"You know, Amanda, you have a very nice way of working things out. Perhaps we should ask Micah to stay for the weekend."

"Don't push it, Carrie. Moving to an apartment would be inconvenient as hell. We'll have to be as subtle in the rest of our matchmaking as we were in asking Micah to dinner. Don't you think we were subtle?"

"Oh, definitely. Poor Blythe never suspected a thing, did she?"

"Poor Blythe" stood in the center of her bedroom, her brown eyes stormy as she reviewed the conversation she'd just had with her aunts. *Damnation!* For a moment she considered changing into a pair of jeans and a sweatshirt, then getting in her car and going to a friend's place or simply driving for an hour or two. Yes, she told herself, that was exactly what she should do, and leave her darling aunties with *their* dinner guest. It would serve them right—and Micah, too.

But even as she considered the idea and desperately wanted to put thought into action, she knew she wouldn't. Micah had already accused her of being a coward where he was concerned. If she were to leave, it would merely reinforce that accusation and give him something else to hang over her head. Yet the urge for revenge was still lurking within her. Revenge against her aunts, who had compounded the problem, and against Micah, who had initiated the problem.

A sudden gleam appeared in her eyes as she walked over to one of the three floor-to-ceiling windows in her bedroom and stared out over the grounds of Greenleigh. There weren't many options open to her at the moment, but of one thing she was certain: her aunts, being sticklers for propriety—especially when there were guests—would be dressed to the nines when they admitted Micah. Blythe turned, her chin thrust forward belligerently, and walked over to the massive armoire that served as a closet.

Some forty-five minutes later, a small jean-clad figure, the upper part of whose body was covered by a voluminous tie-dyed T-shirt, turned her head at the sound of Amanda's voice floating across the grounds.

Blythe, who was kneeling in the dark, rich dirt of the flowerbed and attacking the sprinkling of weeds and grass that dared show their ugly heads, jabbed viciously at the earth with the sturdy hand spade. The weeds and grass had become miniature Micahs, and she was systematically removing each and every one.

"Coming, Aunt Amanda," she replied in a sweet voice. She stood, then looked down at the dirt-encrusted knees of her jeans and the even worse condition of her worn sneakers. Perfect, she silently congratulated herself. Blythe returned the hand spade to the shed that housed the garden tools, wiped her hands on her hips for good measure, and then walked to the house.

The moment she opened the back door, she could hear the deep murmur of Micah's voice coming from the kitchen. "How sweet," she murmured viciously, letting the door slam shut behind her with considerable force. With head held high, she marched through the pantry into the kitchen.

Micah was holding a tureen into which Aunt Carrie was carefully ladling the gumbo. Amanda was darting back and forth from kitchen to dining room, a pleased smile on her face. "I'm sorry if I've kept you waiting," Blythe told the cozy threesome, all of whom turned and stared at her. Her aunts looked aghast, while Micah's mouth became a grim line. "But I simply had to take care of that rosebed. The weeds and grass were almost taking it over." She walked over to the counter and reached out with grimy fingers and filched a piece of celery. "Hello again, Micah." She smiled coolly. "You certainly have spent most of today in Mobile, haven't you?"

"It's proving to be such an interesting place, I might decide to build a hotel in the area," Micah replied pleasantly enough, though the look he was subjecting her to more than conveyed his annoyance at her appearance.

"I thought you would have been dressed for dinner by now, Blythe dear." Amanda frowned.

"I am dressed, Aunt Amanda. As soon as I wash my hands I'll be ready." She flashed a bright smile to the people staring at her, then scooted from the room, barely able to contain her laughter at their horrified expressions.

Although, as Blythe knew for a fact, her aunts would never have appeared at the dinner table dressed as she was, both of them— after their initial surprise—carried on as if nothing out of the ordinary had happened. *It's all Micah's fault*, Blythe kept reminding herself as a bowl of dark gumbo was placed before her. If he hadn't taken advantage of

Carrie and Amanda's generosity, she wouldn't have to eat dinner in tight jeans with damp knees. Nor, she thought disgustedly as she glanced at her hands, would she have broken two fingernails.

Quite frankly, she was thinking while the conversation flowed around her that her entire day had been a series of unpleasant events because of Micah. For some reason, known only to him, he'd decided they should pick up their relationship again. That such a thing wasn't possible kept running through her mind; it wasn't possible at all. Her feelings for Micah had once been so intense, she had been physically ill when they broke up. For weeks after finding him in another woman's arms, she'd thought she would die from the pain. Looking back, she was eventually able to see that her feelings had been a mixture of infatuation, love, admiration, and a healthy dose of awe.

He'd been like a god to her. All the men in her circle of friends had been boys at one time in her life. She'd watched their struggles into adolescence with as much amusement as they'd viewed her development into womanhood. And then Micah had entered her life. She silently sighed. He hadn't been struggling to find himself in the scheme of life or to find a career. That had already been accomplished. He was commanding, assured, and incredibly masculine, and as a successful hotel builder and owner, he'd already made his mark in the corporate world. In her heart, with youthful fantasy that she now remembered with intense embarrassment, she had placed him on a pedestal.

"Don't you agree, Blythe?"

"I'm sorry, Aunt Carrie," she said, blinking at her aunt. "What did you say?"

"I was telling Micah how lovely it is down by the stream. Though we may still have an occasional frost, the violets have already burst into bloom. Why don't you take him out for a walk over the grounds, dear?"

Again three pairs of eyes focused on Blythe, two loving and caring, the other mocking, daring her to do as her aunt suggested.

"I'm sure Micah isn't interested in wildflowers, Aunt Carrie." Blythe smiled. "Besides, I think it's my turn to clear the table, isn't it?"

"You did it last night," Amanda chimed in, then waited expectantly for the next excuse.

"Perhaps you're in a hurry?" Blythe looked stonily at Micah, making no pretense now of hiding her displeasure with the idea of escorting him about.

"I adore wildflowers," he said with maddening ease, "and I have all the time in the world." He smiled.

"Oh." Blythe calmly folded her napkin and laid it beside her plate, then pushed back her chair. "In that case, we'd better get started. It's almost dark."

Any idea she had of hurriedly rushing her unwanted guest through a quick tour of the grounds and back to his car were immediately dashed the moment they reached the wide veranda that covered three sides of the house. As she prepared to practically run down the steps, she felt the restraining grip of Micah's hand grasping her shoulder.

"Not so fast, honey," he said. "I want the whole tour, slowly, not rushed." The pressure on her shoulder increased as he turned her around to face him. "Was it necessary to embarrass your aunts at dinner?"

"My relationship with Carrie and Amanda is my own affair," Blythe told him.

"They're also two very nice ladies, and I care for them very much. In the future," he warned, "I'd suggest that if you have an axe to grind with me, you leave them out of your petty revenge."

Blythe twisted out of his grasp, almost losing her balance as she did so. "There wouldn't have been any need for revenge, petty or otherwise, if you hadn't taken advantage of their friendship. You knew I didn't want to see you again, Micah, but with your usual habit of getting your way, you came anyway."

"Why does seeing me bother you so much?" he asked. They left the steps and began walking toward the tiny stream that ran through the back part of the grounds. "Do you get this upset when Talbot drops by?"

"I don't like being reminded of making a fool of myself," she said honestly. "And that's what I did with you. As for Talbot, he's far more considerate."

"How nice," Micah replied harshly. "Was it kindness that made him start sleeping around only a few weeks after your wedding? Was it consideration for your feelings that created a situation where his fiancée was under the impression that you were his mistress?"

Blythe stopped as if she'd hit a brick wall and stared incredulously at him. "How did you know about that?"

"Never mind how I know." Micah gestured

dismissively with one large hand, his face un-yielding. "What makes me mad as hell is the fact that you insist on treating me like dirt because you think I was unfaithful to you, while you remain friendly with your ex-husband, who was definitely unfaithful to you. Would you care to tell me how you can justify your actions?"

"Believe it or not, Micah, I'm under no obligation to justify anything to you," Blythe said in a tired voice. "If I misjudged you, then I'm sorry."

Micah stared down at her, his expression almost comical with surprise. "I don't believe it. This is the first time in almost two years that you've even remotely admitted that you were wrong. And you were, you know," he said huskily. "I wasn't unfaithful to you, Blythe."

"Then why didn't you put up some sort of struggle?" Blythe coolly inquired. "Why were you taking a shower with that blonde all snug and warm in your bed? Why did you come prancing into your bedroom with nothing but a towel around your waist when you knew she was there? I could go on, but what's the point?"

"All right," Micah said, his gaze stormy. "I

made a huge mistake. Does that make you happy?"

"Not particularly," Blythe said quietly. "What I felt for you was something that would never have worked anyway, Micah. I was like someone on drugs, racing madly about and expending endless energy. Eventually I would have burned out."

"That's a lot of garbage," he muttered. "What we had was beautiful."

"For you, perhaps," Blythe pointed out. "In me, you had a willing subject, a slave who hung on to your every word, who looked at you with about six inches of gauze covering her eyes." Blythe tipped her head slightly. "I've thought about it quite a bit, and I don't think any man could have lived up to the image I'd created of you in my mind. I'd cast you as some immortal being, and we both know you're not, don't we?"

Micah looked out over the gently flowing stream they were approaching, his gaze thoughtful. "I'd be lying if I said I was unaware of the way you felt. It was a heady experience. But I think with time we could have worked things out. Unfortunately, Stephen's unexpected arrival made that impossible. I lost you, and I've never gotten over it. I want you back, Blythe."

"But we can't go back to what we had, Micah," she said patiently. And for the first time in a long time, she found she wasn't angry with him. "We've changed. We might not even like each other now."

"Do you hate me?"

"No."

"Are you indifferent to me?"

"No."

"Doesn't that tell you something?"

"You're pushing it, Micah. I don't want that same desperate kind of love again. It was exhausting. Besides," she admitted, "I still resent the fact that you let a situation such as I found you in happen. In your business, there'll always be women waiting to jump into your bed. You just naturally attract them, and I could never accept those kinds of casual relationships."

Blythe was rather surprised to learn during the remainder of the evening and the following morning that thinking about Micah had become slightly less painful. Their talk had enabled her to voice some of the old hurts that had haunted her for so long.

Around noon, as she hurried from one customer to another, she wondered who had ever been so foolish as to think up such a thing as a sale.

"Pretty hairy, huh?" Cathleen Conley, the part-time sales clerk, groaned as she joined her boss at the cash register.

"I'll say," Blythe heartily agreed. "Are you going out for lunch?"

Cathleen was good, dependable help, and Blythe knew she was lucky to have found her. Cathleen was nineteen, a student, and a very pretty girl. She'd dropped out of college during the fall, unsure of what she wanted to do. At the moment she was working part-time in her father's real estate office and for Blythe while trying to make up her mind about a career.

"I brought a sandwich. How about you?"

"So did I. Did you sell that red dress?"

"And the navy blue one we thought we would have to eat."

"That calls for a celebration indeed," Blythe grinned. "By the way, I put a couple of dresses back for you in the usual place. Look at them when you get a chance."

"I already have." Cathleen grinned. "It'll take me months to pay for them. Oh, look."

She nodded toward the entrance. "Here come your aunts. I can't imagine them going through those condominiums so quickly."

"Neither can I," said Blythe. "Judging by their faces, it must have been a disappointing trip. In fact"—she frowned—"they look terrible." She went forward to meet the two women, concern written on her face. "Aunt Carrie? Aunt Amanda? Is something wrong?"

"He seemed like such a nice man, dear," a dazed Carrie muttered as she clutched Blythe's arm. "It happened so quickly."

"Be thankful it was quick," an equally shaken Amanda said quietly.

"Who was a nice man?" Blythe asked. "And what was it that happened so quickly?" Blythe led her aunts into the stockroom at the back of the boutique, then suggested they sit down.

"How about two cool glasses of water?" a hovering Cathleen asked.

"Please," Amanda nodded, then looked up at her niece. "It was that free offer, you know, a set of steak knives for viewing those new condominiums on the other side of town. We were sitting outside, waiting our turn to be shown through the furnished model, when we were joined by this very nice older man."

71

She paused to accept the water from Cathleen, took a sip, and then continued. "Before long, we were telling him about our fascination with contests, and he told us about his hobby of birdwatching. We told him about the many different birds at Greenleigh and invited him to come down sometime. Suddenly, he looked around, as if searching for someone. Without warning, he jumped to his feet, said it had been nice talking with us, then began running toward the parking lot. In the uproar that followed, we didn't get our steak knives."

"It came out of nowhere," Carrie quietly remarked.

"What did, Aunt Carrie?" Blythe asked.

"The car that killed him," Amanda informed her.

"Killed him? Are you certain?" an astounded Blythe asked. Good heavens! No wonder they were so stunned.

"Dead as a doornail," Carrie intoned. "And the driver of the car never even slowed down."

"I'm so sorry you had to see something like that. I'm also sorry your friend had such an unfortunate accident," Blythe tried to console them.

"Oh, it wasn't an accident, Blythe," said the ever-practical Amanda. "It was quite deliberate. Mr. Johnson was murdered."

"Is that what the police think?"

"They really didn't say." Carrie frowned. "But we saw what happened. Amanda and I tried to give them the details, but you know how some young people are these days. They acted as if we were doddering old fools. As soon as they got our statements, we were dismissed—*dismissed*, mind you."

"Well, I'm sure if you're needed they'll contact you, Aunt Carrie. Frankly, I'm just as happy that you weren't detained. It must have been terrible for both of you."

"It certainly was," Amanda said crisply. "We didn't even get to see the condominiums."

"Oh dear." In spite of poor Mr. Johnson's untimely demise, she found Amanda's remark rather comical. "Perhaps another time. Do you feel like waiting a few minutes for me to get Ainsley in to help Cathleen?"

"What for, dear?" Amanda asked.

"So I can take the two of you home."

Amanda turned to Carrie. "Do you want to go home?"

"No."

73

"Neither do I."

"Oh." Blythe looked from one to the other, concern showing in her face. "In that case, why don't we take these two chairs out front, and you can chat with the customers. Would you like that?"

"Maybe later, dear," Carrie said quietly. "Right now, we'll just sit here and catch our breath. We'll be near you if we need you, won't we?"

"Yes, you will," Blythe murmured huskily as she bent and kissed each softly lined cheek. They were obviously in a state of shock, she thought worriedly. "Call out if you need anything."

On Monday morning, after the fourth phone call from Amanda and Carrie in less than an hour, Blythe decided to call it a day and go home. The aunts, rather than regaining even a small measure of their usual composure after the accident, had become worse. They jumped at the slightest sound, had eaten hardly anything over the weekend, and were unusually quiet. Blythe was worried.

After calling Cathleen and being assured she would come in immediately, Blythe enlisted Ainsley's help until Cathleen arrived; then she went home.

Contrary to her being on the brink of a nervous breakdown, though, she was justly surprised when she entered the house and found her aunts fairly bubbling with excitement.

"Have I got the wrong address?" She smiled as she dropped her purse onto the table. "Can this possibly be the same two women I spoke with several times this morning?"

"Look what came in the mail!" Amanda waved a sheet of crisp stationery toward her. "Carrie and I have won an all-expense-paid two-week vacation at a luxury hotel in Florida. Isn't that exciting?"

"It's marvelous," Blythe agreed while thinking that she would have welcomed fifty more safari hats if it would make them happy. "Does it say when this vacation starts?"

"At our convenience," Carrie chirped brightly. "Amanda and I think now would be an excellent time. But we refuse to go without you."

"Oh, but—" Blythe began to protest, only to have her objections waved aside.

"We really don't like to impose, dear,"

Amanda said quite seriously, "but just this once it would mean so much if you could come with us. We haven't been sleeping well since that terrible accident, and we have come to depend so on you. I'm sure Cathleen and Ainsley wouldn't mind looking after the boutique."

"But Aunt Amanda," Blythe tried again, "this is one of the busiest times of the year. I can't possibly get away."

"Oh, well." Amanda allowed the sheet of paper to drift to the table, her expression as dejected as Carrie's suddenly was. "It was nice for a few minutes."

"It's not—I mean—" Blythe looked from one to the other, her conscience quick to remind her of the times they had put aside important plans of their own in order to indulge her in something she especially wanted. But the boutique would suffer, she told herself. And her aunts were having a terrible time of it right now, a tiny voice reminded her. The boutique could manage without her for a measly two weeks. "When do you want to leave?"

The next afternoon found Blythe and her aunts being graciously welcomed to The

Palms. It was a luxury hotel indeed, located on a small island a mile off the eastern coast of Florida, accessible to the mainland by a causeway.

Amanda and Carrie were shown to a spacious suite, while Blythe found herself ensconced in a lovely room one floor above them. Each accommodation offered a balcony and a beautiful view of the ocean.

After going down to see that Carrie and Amanda were settling in all right, Blythe went back to her room, beginning to feel the first spark of excitement since agreeing to accompany her relatives. She couldn't help but smile as she remembered how neatly they'd brought her around to their way of thinking. In all probability they could have made the trip alone, she reasoned, but what the heck. They weren't exactly young, and she would have worried herself sick wondering about them.

She looked around the beautifully decorated room and smiled. "Forget that your business is going down the tubes, Blythe. This is your first vacation in a long time. Enjoy it!"

With that pleasant thought firmly lodged in her mind, she began to unpack. When a knock came at her door, Blythe had psyched herself into such a euphoric state, she practically floated to the door.

"I'm fine," she called out as she reached for the door, "and the room is terrific."

"I'm glad you approve." Micah smiled lazily at her. He was leaning against the doorjamb, casually dressed in a tan pullover sport shirt and dark brown pants. His blue-gray gaze glided over Blythe in one bold sweep, then came back to her astonished face. "Close your mouth, princess," he chuckled. "You look like a fish."

"Never mind what I look like," Blythe told him the moment she found her tongue. "What are you doing here? This is supposed to be a vacation, and I definitely don't want you ruining it for me."

"Shame on you." Micah moved then. He was through the door and had closed it behind him before Blythe could do more than take two hasty steps back. "I'll be your host for the next two weeks, and I resent those unkind words."

"You own this hotel," she said flatly.

"Of course."

"The contest was a fake?"

"Precisely. I had my PR firm make up a bogus entry form and mail it to Carrie and

Amanda. Since they were the only entrants in the contest, they won hands down."

"At the moment I could gleefully strangle you."

"All's fair in love and war."

"There will be nothing lovelike about it. I resent being tricked, and so, I think, will Amanda and Carrie."

"Not unless you ruin it for them by telling them. Let them enjoy these two weeks. In the meantime, you and I will spend the time getting to know each other again. Wasn't that what you said the other night? That you really didn't know me?"

"I'm known for my rash statements."

"That's too bad, Blythe. I took you at your word. I plan to devote much of my energy to making these next two weeks a time you'll never forget." He leaned forward and dropped a light kiss on her forehead, then turned, opened the door, and left.

Blythe stared dazedly at the door, as if expecting him to return any second. Finally, she turned and looked at her unpacked suitcases, indecision marring her attractive features. If she were to leave, she told herself, it would be a bitter disappointment to her aunts. If she stayed, it could well mean a broken heart for her.

CHAPTER FOUR

With a sense of hopelessness that made her angry rather than depressed, Blythe finished unpacking, then stood in the middle of the room chewing pensively at her bottom lip.

What now? she asked herself. She was fairly certain that if she dared show her face in the lobby, Micah would materialize beside her and sabotage what remained of her day and evening. She knew she couldn't stay in her room indefinitely. Well, she decided, it would probably be best to take her aunts to dinner at one of the restaurants they'd seen near the hotel.

The fact that she would at least be able to enjoy her meal without fear of Micah joining her raised Blythe's spirits slightly. She knew it wasn't a brilliant scheme, but at the moment it was all she could come up with.

After showering and dressing in a cheery yellow sundress, Blythe scooped up her purse and left the room. As she walked down the corridor to the bank of elevators, her thoughts were busy with her plans for the evening. Since she and her aunts were partial to seafood, she thought she would take them to a place Carrie had pointed out. By the time she reached the suite, Blythe was surprised to find herself actually smiling.

Amanda opened the door, and at once Blythe could see that she was excited. "Enjoying yourself, Aunt Amanda?"

"Blythe dear, we've just learned the most exciting news."

"Oh? What is it?" Blythe asked as her arm was grasped and she was pulled into the sitting room.

"You'll never guess who owns this beautiful hotel," Amanda whispered conspiratorially.

For a moment Blythe was tempted to snap that indeed she did know. But the excitement in Amanda's eyes wouldn't let her be so callous. "Who?" she asked instead.

"Micah! Isn't that wonderful? Perhaps during our stay here the two of you can become friends again."

"Aunt Amanda, please don't start out this vacation by trying to play Cupid," Blythe warned her. "Micah and I understand each other perfectly."

"Nonsense, dear," Carrie remarked as she breezed into the room. "If you understand each other so well, then why do you always look as if you're about to bash in his head with a meat cleaver?"

"Or worse," Amanda opined.

"That's all part of our particular kind of understanding." Blythe smiled coolly. "Micah knows I don't trust him an inch, and I know he gets immense pleasure out of harassing me. Let's just leave it at that, shall we?" She walked over and sat down. "Let's talk about dinner. I thought we might go to that seafood restaurant you pointed out, Aunt Carrie, just this side of the causeway. What about it?"

"Oh, I'm afraid we can't this evening, Blythe." Amanda smiled sweetly. "We've all been invited to dine with Micah in his apartment here in the hotel. Doesn't that sound exciting?" she added as she turned and fled from the room, Carrie following close on her heels.

"Just peachy," Blythe muttered stonily, her eyes glittering as she watched her aunts' hurried departure from the sitting room.

Some time later Blythe found herself standing on the balcony of Micah's private apartment. In spite of her determination not to enjoy herself, she was forced to admit that the view was absolutely fantastic.

The still-visible part of the sun, a half-ball of brilliant orange, was quickly disappearing over the horizon, its colorful rays caressing the fleecy clouds and reflecting on the water between the island and the mainland. Blythe knew in her heart that she'd never seen a more beautiful sight. The only problem was, she reasoned mulishly, this particular view belonged to Micah Caine.

She walked farther along the balcony, enjoying the crisp feel of the wind on her face and in her hair as she watched a sailboat skimming along the surface of the small bay that separated the tiny island from the mainland. There were tall palms along the beach, their fringed foliage waving in the wind, and some distance away from the glistening beach that accommodated the hotel guests, she could see the private marina where small craft were kept. The deeper channel also allowed the launches from the different cruise ships to pick up and drop off passengers from The Palms.

"I've been told that this is without a doubt the most beautiful view on the island," Micah said as he came up beside her. "But from the frown on your face, it looks as though you don't agree."

Blythe turned and found him casually leaning against the railing, watching her. "It's beautiful," she confessed, then looked away. "I have no complaints about the view."

"Only me. Right?"

In spite of being annoyed with him, Blythe found herself smiling. "No matter how I answer that, it'll be wrong, won't it?"

"I can't know that until I hear your answer."

"If I say I dislike being here simply because you own the hotel, then I'll sound petty and ridiculous. Especially since it's a beautiful place, and I need the vacation. On the other hand, if I were to tell you that I resent you tricking my aunts—and me—the way you did, I would still sound ridiculous." She turned and faced him. "Though there is one thing I would like to clear up."

"Name it."

"My two weeks are not included in the supposedly free vacation my aunts think they've won. Agreed?"

"Agreed," Micah said shortly. "Though why you insist on being so stubborn about it is beyond me. You've stayed before as my guest. What's so different this time?"

"We were engaged at the time," Blythe reminded him. "And it was at a different hotel. I wouldn't have come even for my aunts if it had been at the same place."

Micah stared at her for several seconds, a wry grin pulling at his lips. "You really do still think I was involved with that woman, don't you?"

"I'd like to say no," Blythe quietly answered, unable to look away from his compelling gaze. "And yet in all honesty I can't. At that time in my life you could do no wrong. To suddenly find you had feet of clay was devastating. However, since I seem to be the only one who thinks you were seeing other women, it's often made me wonder if I overreacted."

"And if you find out that you did overreact, what then?"

"I can't see into the future, Micah. The decision I made—right or wrong—changed both our lives. I'd be less than truthful with you if I were to agree to fall in with your plans for us to pick up where we left off. I've grown up, and the ups and downs that occur in the normal course of my life aren't nearly the crises they once were."

"I'm not sure I like the new you as much as I liked the starry-eyed girl I used to know. She was far easier to deal with and wasn't so inclined to argue." Micah frowned.

"Poor Micah." Blythe smiled teasingly. "You don't like it when things don't go your way, do you?"

"No," he said bluntly. "Especially when those things concern the woman I love."

"I don't want to hear about your love, Micah," Blythe said, turning from gently teasing to very serious. "That was part of our problem. I had neither the experience nor the maturity to deal with you. You swept me off my feet, and," she ruefully admitted, "I didn't do a single thing to stop you."

"Do you think it would be different now?" he asked coolly. This wasn't working out at all as he'd planned. He didn't like the new image Blythe was attempting to project, nor the cold, clinical way she was discussing what they'd once shared.

"I know it would be," she said firmly. She looked toward the door leading into the sitting room of his apartment. "Shouldn't we join Amanda and Carrie?"

Micah allowed his head to tip forward slightly, then reached out and lightly grasped her arm. "Certainly. But I think it only fair to warn you, Blythe: I'm not in the least impressed with this sophisticated veneer you're hiding behind. There are two very important things you haven't considered."

"What?" Blythe asked warily.

"That thing commonly referred to as chemistry between two people, and the heart. Should I elaborate?" he asked huskily just as they reached the doorway.

Blythe looked up and smiled. "Since I'm sure there will be other discussions about both matters, I'll wait."

Amanda and Carrie looked at the approaching couple and smiled. "Isn't this a fantastic place to spend two weeks, Blythe?" Amanda asked cheerfully.

"Yes, Aunt Amanda, it really is," Blythe responded warmly as she sat down next to her aunt on the cream colored sofa. "But what really amazes me is that out of all the different resort hotels in this area, the two of you were lucky enough to win a vacation at one of Micah's hotels."

"Amanda and I were just discussing that when you and Micah came back in," Carrie spoke up. "For the life of us, we can't remember which contest it was that offered this particular prize."

"Perhaps Micah can shed some light on the mystery," Blythe innocently suggested, her brown eyes sparkling as she regarded their host. Let's see him get out of that, she was thinking.

"Er—my PR gal takes care of all the promotions connected with advertising." Micah smiled pleasantly. "She's quite an asset to my company. Always coming up with some clever idea to promote the chain. She's a marvelous woman—simply marvelous," he emphasized, and Blythe knew that was for her benefit.

"I'm so glad to see that you aren't afraid to put women in positions of authority, Micah," Carrie said approvingly. "Only a really confident man would do that and then not be afraid to praise her. Don't you agree, Blythe?"

"Oh, indeed," Blythe purred, doing her

best not to laugh. "I'm sure Micah will have several stars added to his crown for giving us lowly females a boost up the corporate ladder."

"Nicely put, dear." Carrie patted her hand as if Blythe were six years old. She turned back to Micah. "How is your brother?"

"Stephen is fine. I finally talked him into coming to work for me. In fact, you'll probably get to see him before you leave. He's due back in a couple of days. He's taken over one of the bungalows on the grounds for his home."

"How nice—for both of you," Blythe said. "Is he still as fond of partying as he used to be?" There was a steely quality about the look she was directing toward Micah.

"I think you'll find Stephen hasn't changed much." Micah was thinking he would personally murder his brother if the slightest bit of confusion regarding women arose while Blythe was at the hotel.

The silent appearance in the dining-room doorway of a white-coated waiter caught Micah's attention. "Dinner is served, Mr. Caine."

"Thank you, Joseph." Micah stood and saw first Carrie and then Amanda to their feet.

"This way, ladies." He turned his head and grinned at Blythe. "If you'd care to wait, I'd be happy to seat your aunts and then come back for you."

"How kind," Blythe murmured politely. "But I think I'm capable of tottering along by myself. Perhaps Stephen will hurry up and arrive. Then you won't find yourself so out-numbered."

A quelling stare was all the response she got to that remark, which she knew would draw sparks.

The dinner, consisting of several seafood dishes, drew praise from Amanda, Carrie, and Blythe. Both aunts took wine with the meal, and by the time dessert was finished their small white heads were almost nodding at the table.

"Oh, dear," Carrie murmured in embar-rassment after trying unsuccessfully to smother a yawn. "I'm afraid the wine and such a delicious dinner have made me sleepy."

Blythe grinned. "Do you suppose it could possibly have anything to do with the fact that you're tired from the trip? We were all up very early this morning."

"Yes, we were," Amanda agreed. "Thank

you, Micah, for a lovely dinner. I do hope you will understand if we don't stay and visit, but if we were to do that, we'd probably embarrass ourselves by falling off to sleep."

"I understand perfectly." He smiled, then pushed back his chair and rose to his feet. "Let me get Joseph to see you to your suite."

After watching the stalwart Joseph usher her aunts out the door, Blythe saw Micah lock the door, then turn and walk back into the room. While he was moving, he removed his jacket and tie, then turned back the snowy cuffs of his white shirt.

When he finally came to a stop in front of Blythe, he in no way resembled the courteous, smiling man who had been so attentive and charming at dinner. The man staring down at her was sending out the most sensual messages, messages that were reaching out and quietly encircling her like an intangible force.

Though his stance wasn't overtly threatening, Blythe felt a tiny scamper of fear course along her spine. Her gaze was drawn to his rigid features, which only moments ago had been soft and smiling. Her eyes slid down past the open V of his shirt and the dark blond hair on his chest to the solid firmness of his thighs.

He looked like a man ready to do battle, and for the first time in her life Blythe knew what it meant to be really frightened.

"Would you care for something else to drink?" Micah asked the question so softly that Blythe gave a slight start at the sound of his voice.

"N-no." She quickly shook her head. She moved forward and to the left of him in an effort to get to her feet without the move bringing her face to face with Micah. "I hate to eat and run," she said breathlessly, "but I don't think my aunts are the only ones who need an early night."

But she never made it to her feet. Micah dropped down beside her, one long arm finding its way across the front of her waist and neatly pressing her back against the cushions of the sofa.

"I can remember times when we stood at the window together and watched the sun rise," he said huskily. "I don't recall you being interested in sleeping then."

"Age," Blythe croaked. "I'm older now, and I need an incredible amount of sleep." She tried squirming out from beneath his heavy arm, but in the scramble her breasts brushed against his warm flesh and she stopped, silently cursing the traitorous hardening of her nipples at the contact. Her hands found leverage on the cushioned seat, and she slowly eased backward.

"Having problems, honey?" Micah was watching her, his lips twitching as he tried not to laugh.

"No problems," Blythe countered offhandedly in a rush of breath that resembled that of a wheezing asthmatic.

"Then kiss me."

"Why?"

"Because it's something we'll both enjoy."

"Use discipline, Micah, and deny yourself. It will make you a bigger person."

"I'm big enough now."

"I feel I must warn you that I'm suffering from a rare tropical disease, transmissible only by kissing."

"I'll risk it."

"I'd rather kiss a toad."

"I know, dear. That's because you're only happy with one of your own kind. I, on the other hand, have a special fondness for toads. Especially ones with flashing dark eyes and very kissable lips." His other hand slipped behind her head and held it immobile.

A barely audible no floated past Blythe's

lips; it was absorbed by Micah's hovering mouth as he took possession not only of her lips but of her warm, trembling body as well. His touch was electric; his fingers were magnetic probes that sought out all the familiar places he'd known in the past. Blythe felt herself becoming dizzy from lack of breath, but for some reason she didn't panic. Her body felt as if it were floating, yet never in her life had she been more aware of sound, of the textures of skin and hair, or of movement, than at that moment.

When she felt Micah raise his head, she opened her eyes and stared dazedly at him, her expression almost one of bewilderment at the interruption.

"Stay with me tonight," he whispered, his thumb slowly tracing the swollen softness of her mouth. "Stay and help me recapture the time when there were only the two of us in a golden world."

Blythe momentarily closed her eyes against that hypnotic gaze pulling at her, knowing that if she didn't move—and move fast— Micah would get exactly what he wanted. She couldn't allow that to happen, she told herself. Even if she had originally misjudged him, he should never have been in that damn bedroom with that blonde.

"I don't care to renew old memories, Micah. I'd much rather build new ones. Besides, if my aunts needed me during the night, they wouldn't know where to find me."

"There'll be other moments, darling, I promise you that. In the meantime, I can wait," he said huskily.

CHAPTER FIVE

The ringing of the telephone roused Blythe from a sound sleep. It took several fumbling seconds before she was able to find the receiver and hold it against her ear.

"Hello?" she murmured sleepily.

"Blythe?" Amanda's voice sounded excited. "Are you ready for breakfast?"

"Breakfast," Blythe repeated dully, then forced her eyes open. "What time is it?"

"Seven o'clock, and it's a beautiful day. Carrie and I have been up for nearly two hours, but we thought we would let you sleep late."

"How kind," Blythe muttered, and closed her eyes again. "This is supposed to be a vacation, Aunt Amanda. Why are you getting up so early?" Lord, Blythe was thinking, if getting up before daylight was going to be the established routine for the next two weeks, she would head back to Mobile right after breakfast.

"Because the early bird catches the worm, child," Amanda informed her.

"I don't care for worms, Aunt Amanda. Besides, the only worm I know is Micah. Why don't you call and wake him? He'd probably be delighted to have breakfast with you and Aunt Carrie."

"Nonsense," Amanda continued, not daunted in the least by her niece's lack of enthusiasm. "Once you get up and start stirring around, you'll feel wonderful. As for Micah, I'm sure we *will* see him at breakfast."

Blythe decided not to argue the point. She'd long ago discovered that singlemindedness was a trait with which both her aunts were generously blessed. "I'll meet you in the dining room in twenty minutes, okay?"

"Fine, dear."

After replacing the receiver, Blythe gave a loud groan of frustration. At that moment, she decided that the first order of business when she arrived at breakfast would be to establish a few rules for the coming weeks, the first one being that each of them could make individual plans, like sleeping late.

With that idea firmly set in her mind, which would save her from more early morning calls, Blythe reasoned, she scrambled from the bed and began to dress.

After leaving her room, she walked to the elevator, where she had to wait for several minutes. Blythe found herself gazing at the comfortable two-seater couch placed there for the guests' convenience. The ice and drink machines were tastefully encased in wood-grained exteriors that blended nicely with the attractive cream wallpaper with narrow blue and tan stripes. The carpet was also tan and afforded one a luxurious and safe footing.

Blythe wondered how many hotels Micah owned now. At the time of their engagement, it had been five. She'd heard since then that he'd opened two or three more on the islands, as well as one in Acapulco. When the elevator door opened, she stepped inside. Regardless of their personal differences, she knew of no fault that could be found with his role as host to the thousands of customers that passed through his hotels each year.

Amanda and Carrie were sitting at a table

that could be easily seen from the doorway. Blythe made her way toward them, relieved to see them looking so refreshed. The accident they'd witnessed at the condominium seemed to have been forgotten—or at least it wasn't preying on their minds, as it had at first.

"You're both looking chipper this morning. What plans have you made for the day?" She smiled as she slipped into a chair and reached for the orange juice they'd ordered for her.

"We're going on a cruise," Carrie told her. She pointed to a brochure beside her plate. "Three days touring the islands. Doesn't that sound exciting?"

Blythe looked at the sleek lines of the cruise ship and nodded approvingly, momentarily forgetting her resolve to set the rule of individual plans. "Sounds delightful. When do we leave?"

"*We* leave at one o'clock today." Carrie glanced uncomfortably at Amanda, then back at her niece. "We'll be back before you even miss us, dear."

"What do you mean, 'miss you'? I like the idea of a cruise. I can be packed and ready to go within thirty minutes." Blythe smiled.

"Don't worry," she assured them, "I wouldn't dream of making you late getting to the ship."

"Well, that's nice, dear," Carrie said earnestly, "and we appreciate your concern. But the fact of the matter is, we'd like to go alone."

"Alone?" Blythe asked, surprised. "Why?"

"We think it only fair that this vacation be equally as pleasant for you as for us, Blythe." Amanda was joining the conversation. "We talked it over and decided that we weren't going to make a nuisance of ourselves. This is an excellent time for each of us to go and do things on our own. Besides, with us out of the way, you'll have more time to spend with Micah."

Blythe slowly shook her head. "When will the two of you get it through your heads that I don't want to spend more time with Micah?"

Amanda reached out and patted her hand. "Of course you do, dear. It's just that stubborn Donaldson pride that's keeping you and him apart. Believe me, we understand perfectly."

A look of complete frustration captured Blythe's face. She looked helplessly about as though searching for some words that would convince her relatives that she wasn't *dying* to get Micah Caine back.

"There is nothing to understand," she tried again. "If you want to go on the cruise without me, fine, but I'm certainly not staying so that I'll be alone with Micah."

"When my Albert and I were first interested in each other, we were always at cross-purposes," Amanda consoled Blythe. "You'll find the course of true love has many twists and turns, but you must persevere. Things will work out for you."

"I'm sure they will." Blythe sighed defeatedly. "So," she said brightly, determined to change the subject, "what made you decide on a cruise?"

"Well," Carrie began, "as you will recall, last summer we discussed taking a cruise, but after that trip we took to the mountains and the one to San Francisco, we decided to wait. When we arrived yesterday and saw the brochures listing the various things to do in the area, we both decided this short cruise would be first." She leaned closer to Blythe and spoke quietly. "You know, dear, this will be the first time either of us has been on a ship. That's why we decided on just three days. We might not enjoy it at all. Seasickness, you know."

101

"Are you sure you don't want me to go with you in case something like that happens?"

"Positive," Amanda said strongly. "We want you to enjoy yourself without having to worry about us. Besides, we've been talking to several others who will be along, and they tell us it's an excellent setting to meet some interesting men."

"Oh—of course," Blythe nodded, conjuring up images of her aunts returning to the hotel with a line of eligible men strung out behind them. "Just be careful," she warned, "shipboard romances are famous for fizzling out once you're back ashore."

"I'm sure that's true, dear, but just think of the excitement while it's in full swing." Carrie smiled. "Oh, by the way, as soon as the dress shop here in the hotel opens, you must come and help us select a couple of outfits suitable for deck wear."

"What do you have in mind?" Blythe asked cautiously. From the amount of luggage they'd brought with them, she couldn't think of a single thing they needed to buy. "You both have several pairs of nice slacks that would do beautifully."

"Really, Blythe." Amanda frowned. "We don't want to wear slacks all the time. We were thinking more along the line of some shorts, and perhaps a pair of culottes."

"Shorts?"

"Well, of course," Carrie chimed in. "You don't want us looking dated, do you?"

"Definitely not," Blythe assured them. Oh Lord, she thought, the idea of a cruise had made them go slightly bonkers. "As soon as we finish eating, we'll head right over to the shop. Have you told Micah your plans?"

"No," Amanda said thoughtfully. "I do hope his feelings won't be hurt by us leaving him for a few days."

"Oh, I'm sure he won't mind in the least," Blythe assured her. Why should he? she thought as they rose and headed for the lobby. With her aunts away, Micah would become her own personal shadow.

The amount of time her aunts spent in the dress shop had Blythe wondering if there were a hidden camera somewhere that was recording a prank being played on her. That, or her aunts had lost all sense of reason.

"Don't you think that blouse is a little bright, Aunt Amanda?" she asked as her aunt removed a brilliant red top from one of the racks and studied it.

"Nonsense," Amanda waved one hand dismissively. "I want to be seen, Blythe, not to sit in a corner knitting."

"Well, you'll certainly accomplish your goal if you buy that little number." Blythe sighed, then did a double-take when she spied Carrie sauntering out of the dressing room clad in a blue, one-piece shorts outfit. Though it came to her knees, it was still by far the most flamboyant garment—aside from her feather-trimmed robes—that Blythe had ever seen her aunt wear.

"Aunt Carrie," she murmured as she hurried forward, "are you sure you want something as youthful as this?"

"Why, certainly I do," Carrie spiritedly replied. "Amanda and I decided we want these next three days to be memorable, dear. If you want to play the game, you have to have the equipment with which to beat the competition." She looked down at the outfit she was wearing and smiled. "I think this will do nicely."

"Um, exactly what game do you have in mind?" Blythe asked, once the spinning in her head had stopped.

"Fun," she was told. "Amanda and I decided we weren't going to be relegated to some comfortable deck chair in a corner. This cruise caters to people our age, and we intend to make the most of it."

"I see," Blythe replied faintly as Carrie walked over to get her sister's opinion. Though Blythe knew she would worry about them, she had to admit that there was something about both Amanda and Carrie's attitudes that she admired.

"It's a bit early to be shopping, isn't it?"

Blythe turned and found herself looking straight into Micah's blue-gray gaze. His hair was still damp from the shower, and she could see a tiny razor nick on his chin. He looked strong and vital and more than capable of tackling any or all problems that might occur during the day.

"I'm afraid I'm not the one adding gold to your coffers." Blythe smiled. "The aunts have decided to become the belles of the ball during their cruise. The ship's crew may never be the same again."

Just then, Micah caught sight of Carrie, Amanda, and the young sales clerk, who appeared to be having as much fun helping the two ladies as they were making their selections. "I see what you mean." He grinned after getting a closer look at Carrie's outfit. "Do you think they'll be all right going by themselves?"

"How did you know they were going alone?" Blythe asked suspiciously. She'd been wondering all along if he'd had a hand in this sudden arrangement.

"They called last night and asked me if I could pull a couple of strings and get them included. The deadline was the day before yesterday."

"I suppose I should be pleased with your efforts. I've never seen them happier. As for them going alone, I only hope the captain and the crew are well rested. If their other passengers are half as energetic as my aunts, they're in for the surprise of their lives."

"Their absence is going to leave you with a lot of free time on your hands," Micah said softly. "Any plans?"

"Any more cruises available?" she asked cheekily.

"Not a single one." He grinned. "But don't worry," he murmured as he leaned over and brushed her temple with his lips, "I have some wonderful ideas when it comes to entertaining my guests. Especially one with dark, curly hair and lovely brown eyes."

"Oh, I'm sure you do," Blythe murmured,

smiling in spite of herself. "Perhaps we should get together and pool our ideas—when I find myself getting bored, that is."

"Of course," Micah drawled huskily, the twinkle in his eyes almost causing Blythe to forget that she was supposed to be annoyed with him. "I have an appointment now, but I'll go with you and your aunts when the launch arrives to pick them up."

The noonday sun was at its brightest, causing Blythe, in spite of the dark glasses she was wearing, to shield her eyes with her hand as she watched Amanda and Carrie board the sleek cruise ship.

"Don't worry about them," Micah said. He was watching Blythe and could tell that she was concerned.

"I'm not worried about their safety as much as their expectations. They've been talking about going on a cruise for ages."

"Then why haven't they?"

"I honestly don't know. At any rate, once I got over the shock of them actually going and the wild wardrobes they chose for the occasion, I was all for it."

"Since it's unlikely that they're hanging over the ship's rail waving to us, why don't we head back to the hotel and have something cool to drink?"

"Sounds like a good idea," Blythe agreed, then quickly added, "but don't let me take you away from something important, Micah. Just because Amanda and Carrie aren't here doesn't mean you have to spend every waking minute with me."

His hand at her elbow tightened as they turned and walked toward the peculiar-looking vehicle with wide tires that was used to take guests to and from the marina. "Do you lie awake at night and try to think up ways to annoy me, Blythe?" he asked harshly.

"Is that what you really think?" she asked, surprised.

"That's what I really think," Micah mimicked sarcastically. After seeing that she was belted into the seat, he got in beside her, started the engine, and roared off across the sand toward the hotel.

Blythe sat beside him, not wanting to pursue the conversation, yet oddly curious as to why he'd suddenly become angry. She was beginning to feel a sense of normalcy in being with Micah again. It had seemed the most natural thing in the world for him to drive her and her aunts to the marina. She'd already promised to have a drink with him, and now she was sitting beside him, wondering what he was thinking. Becoming caught up in Micah's feelings would only be an exercise in frustration, she reasoned, deciding to ignore his mood.

Instead of going into the lounge when they reached the hotel, Micah led Blythe to a shaded table beside the pool. A waiter hurried over and took their order, which Micah gave without consulting Blythe. When she pointed this out to him, he regarded her levelly.

"A piña colada loaded with fresh pineapple used to be one of your favorite drinks. Have you developed a distaste for it during the past two years?"

"No."

"Then why the lecture?"

"I wasn't lecturing you, Micah," Blythe replied. "I was merely pointing out that you hadn't bothered to ask me what I wanted."

"Would you care for something else?"

"No."

"I apologize. Does that make you feel better?"

"Not especially."

"Ah." Micah grinned. "Now I'm beginning

to understand. You're itching for a fight, aren't you? If I were to prostrate myself at your feet, would it make you feel any better?"

"Gee, I don't know." Blythe grinned impishly. "Why don't you try it and let me see how it affects me?"

For a moment Micah simply stared at her. His expression was tender, and Blythe could feel the fine hairs on the back of her neck standing on end.

"I've sat by this pool many times, mostly late at night, and tried to think of ways of getting you here," he finally said.

"Micah, please." Blythe slowly shook her head. "Don't complicate things for me."

"If loving you is a complication, then I'm afraid you'll just have to adjust," he said quietly. They were sitting at opposite sides of the table, but to Blythe, the quiet throbbing of feeling coursing between them made space unimportant. His eyes and his very nearness were caressing her as intimately and lovingly as if his hands were actually touching her.

The arrival of the waiter with their drinks and a message for Micah that he was wanted on the phone prevented Blythe from having to stumble through a response. She sat back and sipped the piña colada, her eyes on Micah as he motioned for the young man to plug in the phone, then raised the receiver to his ear.

After several minutes of listening to the conversation with Ric Sutherland, the current star in the Emerald Room of The Palms, Blythe decided that it would be to her advantage to make her escape. She wasn't ready for a heart-to-heart talk with Micah, especially when he would only look straight at her and tell her how much he loved her.

CHAPTER SIX

On reaching her room, the first thing Blythe did was change from the white shorts she was wearing to a pair of beige slacks and a sleeveless brown cotton sweater. She reached for a large straw purse that was reminiscent of one of Amanda's favorites. Into it she stuffed a light windbreaker, her billfold, and a pair of tennis shoes in case she decided to do any walking. She grabbed her keys, then stole quietly from the room. Ten minutes later she was in her car crossing the causeway to the mainland, then turning left and driving down the coast.

As she drove, Blythe found herself relaxing for the first time since her arrival at The

Palms. Though her initial reason for leaving the hotel for a few hours had been to get away from Micah, she knew in her heart that it would be time that she needed to try and sort out her feelings for him.

She had to admit that she was at a loss to understand the antagonism that was always simmering just beneath the surface whenever she saw Micah. Constant arguing wasn't in her nature. Surely, she told herself, after almost two years she should be able to put the past behind her. Why couldn't she?

Memories of her brief marriage drifted through her mind, especially the now-comical scene with Talbot's girlfriend. After recovering from the shock of learning that her husband was leading a double life, Blythe had continued on without any outwardly visible signs of stress. Emotionally, it had hurt her. No, she frowned, that wasn't exactly the truth. It hadn't hurt her as much as it had humiliated her. Yet, she reasoned as she drove along the coast, even when the dissolution of her marriage had become fact, there was no comparison between that and the emptiness, the loneliness she'd felt when she discovered that Micah had been unfaithful to her.

Since the divorce, she and Talbot had remained friends. Why, she asked herself, couldn't she do the same with Micah? Why was there this secret desire within her to want him to feel the same degree of pain she'd suffered? Could it be that the incident in Micah's suite with the blonde was forcing her to really take a long, hard look at their relationship? Blythe wondered.

Micah had been the most absorbing thing in her life, and she'd rushed foolishly ahead, never stopping to examine the differences in their backgrounds or the separate priorities that dominated their lives. Blythe sighed as she remembered. She'd been fresh out of college, eager to get started in her career. Her aunts had provided the cushion of support that had made her world so secure, so safe. Micah, on the other hand, had been on his own since his early teens. He'd supported himself and Stephen by any means he could find. Through hard work and determination he'd amassed a fortune. So perhaps, Blythe reasoned, the incident that had shattered her hadn't been that important to him. Yet she knew that living with a man who had such a casual approach to relationships would never satisfy her. She needed a commitment, strong and binding, from a man, and she was afraid that Micah, surrounded by the type of people that made up his life, wasn't capable of making such a commitment.

Blythe passed the remainder of the afternoon feeling curiously adrift. The same depth of loneliness stayed with her as she found a deserted stretch of beach and walked along it. It was still with her when she got in the car and headed back toward The Palms. Even a prolonged visit to the outskirts of a small town where a number of artists had formed a colony failed to drive away the sense of finality surrounding her thoughts where Micah was concerned.

For once, she was really looking at the situation. She accepted that her own behavior before and after the breakup had been childish. Seeing Micah as often as she had for the past few days was acting as a long-needed catalyst. She could no longer place all the blame squarely on his shoulders. Blythe knew now that she'd been like a child, naïvely looking at life through the eyes of storybook characters. She'd wanted a knight in shining armor, complete with a white horse and all the trimmings. When she found she'd gotten a human being instead, she'd panicked, unable to cope with the unpredictability of a mere mortal.

She sighed ruefully. Her banishment of Micah from her life now appeared foolish, even immature. She'd wanted revenge. Even her marriage to Talbot had been a further extension of that desire for revenge.

So what now? she asked herself.

She could always go to Micah and tell him what she was feeling, her conscience pointed out. But Blythe slowly shook her head at that thought. Resuming a love affair with Micah wasn't really what she wanted—at least, she didn't think it was. Oh, she was still intensely aware of him; her body responded to his touch without forethought or design. But that wasn't enough. She wasn't looking for fairy tales anymore.

As Blythe entered the lobby of the hotel and made her way toward the bank of elevators, she heard her name being called in a deep, angry voice.

She turned and saw Micah bearing down on her, his expression dark and ominous.

"Is something wrong?" she asked when he came to a halt beside her.

"Where the hell have you been all afternoon?" he charged like an angry bull. "It's almost seven o'clock."

"So it is." Blythe smiled. "I'm sorry if you

116

were worried. It seemed like the perfect day to do a little exploring on my own."

At that moment one of the elevators opened and Blythe stepped inside and pressed the button, rather amused by the still-glaring giant. He had followed her into the elevator.

"The next time you decide to go exploring," Micah continued his tirade, "at least have the decency to let somebody know."

"Why?" She turned and looked up at him. "Am I supposed to be punching a time clock while I'm here?"

"Don't get flip with me, Blythe," he warned. "I'm in no mood for it."

"Neither am I, Micah," she calmly replied. "I'm one of your guests, remember?"

"The hell you are," he snapped.

The elevator came to a stop at her floor and the door slid open. Blythe breathed a sigh of relief. Instead of allowing Micah to continue with his senseless griping, she turned and placed a firm hand in the middle of his chest at the exact moment he started to step forward. "I do not care to listen to any more of your grumbling," she said firmly. "I've been here less than forty-eight hours, and we've done nothing but fuss. I'm tired. All I want is to go to my room and rest. Now, will you please find some other poor soul to intimidate and leave me alone?"

Micah chewed at the corner of his bottom lip, his penetrating gaze never leaving her face.

"There's something different about you," he said thoughtfully. "Where did you go this afternoon? Who did you see?"

"I'm twenty-six years old, Micah. I don't need your stamp of approval about the people I meet, nor do I need you to take me by the hand and lead me to dinner, then tuck me into bed." She turned and stepped from the elevator. "Good night."

Micah jabbed the close button savagely, his lips compressed into a hard, disapproving line. *Damn stubborn woman!* He'd wanted to spend the afternoon with her, had wanted the two of them to go on a picnic. He leaned back against the wall of the elevator, his hands jammed into the pockets of his pants. Why the hell did he still have this crazy hang-up about Blythe Donaldson? Oh, he freely admitted that he loved her, but it was more than that. In his lifetime he'd known one or two individuals who'd found happiness with a husband or wife while loving another. But with

Blythe it was different. He had no desire whatsoever to share his life with another woman.

The last two years had been pure hell. He'd tried to forget her, tried damned hard. He'd used women as a sexual release and nothing more. Eventually he'd become so disgusted with himself, he had found it difficult even to look in a mirror. That's when he made the decision to get Blythe back. Micah had vowed that he would. Nothing had ever come easy for him, but he loved a good fight. He would soon have her back in his arms and in his bed with his ring on her finger.

She'd handled that little encounter with Micah very nicely, Blythe congratulated herself as she unearthed her room key from the bottom of the large straw purse. Very nicely indeed. Micah had been put off stride, and she had escaped unscathed. The days ahead were looking better and better. She inserted the key, pushed open the door, and gasped.

"What on earth?" Taking a few cautious steps inside, her head moved from side to side as she tried to take in the shambles that greeted her.

Each drawer of the dresser had been left

open. Underwear, pantyhose—every item from the drawers was either hanging over the edges or lying on the carpet. The same treatment had been accorded to her clothes hanging in the dressing room—most of them were now left on the floor. Even her makeup hadn't gone unscathed. Every jar and tube had been opened and the contents probed and smeared like a child's fingerpaints.

Blythe stared dazedly at her luggage and at the savage manner in which the lining had been ripped out; it was hanging in shreds. The bed was a shambles, and the mattress was half off the box spring. Chairs were overturned and lamps were tipped over.

She started to turn and run, then realized that whoever was responsible for the destruction had obviously gone. On very unsteady legs, Blythe made her way over to the telephone and lifted the receiver to dial the front desk.

When a friendly voice answered, she licked her suddenly dry lips. "Er, yes. This is Blythe Donaldson in six-ten. I'm afraid someone has broken into my room. Would you please send up someone from security?"

"Certainly, Ms. Donaldson. But are you all right?" the man quickly asked.

"I'm fine." She laughed shakily. "In fact, I just this moment walked in—fortunately."

"We'll be right there." The line went dead, and Blythe slowly replaced the receiver.

She sat down on one corner of the crazily arranged mattress, still stunned by what she was seeing. Yet as she recovered from the shock, slow anger began to build within her. Nothing like this had ever happened to her before, and she found she didn't like the idea of a total stranger rifling through her belongings. She shivered; the thought made her flesh crawl.

Within minutes, she could hear the muted sounds of voices and footsteps hurrying down the corridor. Micah was the first to enter the room through the still-open door; he was closely followed by two other men. He abruptly halted when he saw the extent of the damage; then he quickly looked at Blythe.

"Are you all right?" he asked gruffly, then walked over and sat down beside her. He reached out and caught one of her hands in a warm grasp.

Blythe nodded. "I'm fine. Just shocked."

Micah took a deep breath and exhaled noisily as he turned and surveyed the room. "I can understand why." He nodded toward the two men who had been moving cautiously about the room. "This is Ben Adams and Ted Wilkerson from security." Both men nodded and smiled.

"The obvious question, Miss Donaldson, is, did you see anyone when you came in?" Ted Wilkerson asked.

"No one." Blythe shook her head. "I rode up in the elevator with Mi—er, Mr. Caine. From there to my door, I didn't see another person."

Micah rose to his feet and walked into the dressing area, where Ben Adams was looking at the counter where the intruder had dumped and smeared Blythe's makeup. "Any ideas, Ben?"

"None." The burly security guard looked baffled. "There hasn't been even one complaint from any of the other guests."

"Well, let's run a discreet check anyway," Micah said. "Several of the guests left on that cruise today, including Miss Donaldson's aunts. Have a look at their rooms." He looked back at Blythe. "Have you been able to figure out if anything is missing?"

She shrugged. "I honestly haven't thought about it. I had my billfold with me, so that's safe." She leaned over and picked up a small, flat, leather-bound box and opened it. The only jewelry she'd brought with her were her mother's pearls and a favorite gold bracelet that had been a gift from, of all people, Micah. She looked up and met his gaze. "My jewelry hasn't been bothered."

She watched as he and the two security men went into a quiet huddle. When they left, Micah turned back to Blythe. "Housekeeping with be up to take care of this," he said, waving his hand toward the confusion. "In the meantime, you'll be moving in with me."

"No."

"What?"

"I said no. I will not be moving in with you."

"That's the silliest damn thing I've ever heard you say." He scowled.

"That's your problem. In the meantime, I'd appreciate it if you could find me another room. I really don't relish the thought of staying in this one."

"Have I suddenly become a carrier of the plague?"

Blythe had to smile. "No, Micah." She tipped her head to one side and regarded him with amusement. "But for the life of me, I can't figure out who I fear more, you or the burglar."

"Then you're finally willing to admit that I'm a threat?" he asked huskily.

"Alarmingly so. But I'm no longer in the market for a knight in shining armor."

"You've wounded me," he replied in feigned remorse.

"But you'll survive, won't you?" she asked curiously.

"Oh, I could, if I set my mind to it," he said softly.

"But?"

"But I've no intention of doing anything so foolish. Will you answer me one question?"

"Certainly."

"Something happened today that's changed you. What was it?"

"I think I grew up," she confessed. "I also stopped blaming you for something I should have been able to handle."

Micah regarded her thoughtfully for a moment. He reached out and gently brushed his knuckles along the delicate line of her jaw. "That's more than I was expecting. I'd grown weary of that look of frozen rejection in your eyes each time we met."

"You might grow just as weary of the new

me." Blythe smiled uneasily, feeling a sudden shyness with him that was uncharacteristic, considering the circumstances. She'd known this man intimately and yet, at this precise moment, she felt as if she were poised on the brink of something new and exciting.

"Never, Blythe," he muttered hoarsely as he enfolded her tenderly in his arms and pressed her head against his chest.

CHAPTER SEVEN

Blythe spent the next hour arranging her things in the new room that had been provided for her.

"I still don't see why you won't move in with me," Micah grumbled as he stood in the center of the room and watched her hang the last of her clothes. "It's not as though we're strangers."

"That's precisely why I won't do as you suggest," Blythe said firmly. "I'd wind up in your bed before the night was over."

"I know." He grinned.

Blythe favored him with a level glare. She reached for her purse and began removing her extra cosmetics; then she placed them on the dressing room counter. "And all this time I thought you were concerned about the emotional trauma I've suffered from finding my room practically destroyed."

"Oh, I am," he informed her as he walked over and stood temptingly close beside her. "In my arms you'd forget all about your trauma."

"How unkind." Blythe grinned. "All you want is my body."

"For a while I thought I was going to have to draw you a picture."

"No picture is necessary, Mr. Caine. As difficult as it may be for you to understand, at the moment I'm more concerned about the fact that only my room and my aunt's room were broken into. Somehow, I'd feel better if there'd been other rooms involved."

"Are you hoping to bankrupt me?" Micah asked lazily.

"With your Midas touch, that's hardly likely," Blythe quipped. "Seriously though, I hope Carrie and Amanda aren't too upset when they get back and learn what's happened."

"If it wasn't for the fact that their luggage and several other items have to be replaced, we wouldn't even have to tell them," Micah said thoughtfully.

"They won't like your having to replace anything that was damaged," Blythe said. "In their estimation you can do no wrong."

"I know." He chuckled. "How do you feel about the matter?"

"I have no such illusions, so I'll spend your money without the slightest qualm."

"Somehow I knew you'd say that. By the way, I had the police come in and check for prints in both rooms. They couldn't find anything. I'd suggest we not mention that to Carrie and Amanda. Just let them think it was one in a rash of petty burglaries. Okay?"

"Okay," Blythe agreed. She folded her arms across her upper body and regarded him with something akin to amusement. "If you're still taking me to dinner, would it be asking too much for you to leave? I'd like to shower and dress."

"I'll wait for you."

"In your apartment or in the dining room?"

"Here."

"That's what I was afraid of." Blythe shrugged. "Oh well, I suggest you get comfortable. I've no intention of hurrying." She walked into the other room and began gathering up fresh underwear and a robe. Then she turned back to the bathroom, where Micah was still leaning against the dressing counter. "You may wait over there," she said, pointing to one of the overstuffed chairs in front of the window. "I haven't gotten so liberal that I take my showers with men present."

"I remember a few times when we used to take showers together. I'd be happy to help recreate that pleasurable experience for you," he drawled, his gaze hooded and unreadable. "In case you've forgotten."

Blythe hadn't forgotten, and the memory of his large hands caressing her as the warm water fell over their naked bodies brought a profusion of color to her cheeks. "I remember," she replied stonily. "On the other hand, I'd think with all your worldly experience that you would have learned something a little different since we broke up. Perhaps something wild and exotic?" She pointed to the chair by the window. "Please?"

Micah took two steps, then stopped. He turned and looked at her, a wry grin pulling at his sensuous mouth. "Wild and exotic, huh? I'll see what I can come up with. Oh, and don't be too long," he added silkily, "or I might be tempted to settle for something rather ordinary like we used to enjoy."

"Out," Blythe ordered him, then slammed the dressing-room door. She quickly went into the bathroom and turned on the shower to drown out his amused laughter. Her shower was hurried too, for she knew that if he chose, Micah wouldn't hesitate to join her. All her quiet rationalizing during the afternoon wasn't doing her much good at the moment, she thought resignedly as she held her face up to the water.

When she'd first left Micah in the elevator, she'd felt positively lightheaded about the way she'd handled him. She'd been firm without resorting to pettiness, determined to treat him like any other man she'd known. The trouble was, she silently acknowledged, she hadn't known any other man as she'd known Micah. Even with Talbot, there'd never been that gut-wrenching surge of emotion that could—and often did—make her feel as if she were being thrown from the top of a mountain, only to be caught and cushioned in a pair of loving arms as she made the descent.

Suddenly, Blythe found her hands going to her head and covering her ears as if to shut out the voice that kept nagging and tormenting her about what had been with Micah. That was behind her, she silently argued, behind her for good. But although those words were sincere, she somehow got the feeling that words wouldn't be enough to save her when Micah's patience ran out.

With a sense of annoyance eating at her for her cowardice, Blythe reached out blindly and turned off the deluge of water. She pushed back the shower door and picked up a large fluffy towel. After patting most of the moisture from her skin, she wrapped the towel around her body, then left the steamy bath for the dressing room. She caught up another small towel and twisted it around her dripping hair. But when she automatically reached for her hair dryer, she remembered that she'd left it on the dresser in the bedroom.

Cute. she frowned at her reflection in the mirror. *Real cute.* Parading before Micah with nothing but a towel wrapped around her would be tantamount to waving the proverbial red flag at a bull. It was too much to hope that he'd gone by now.

Hunger pangs in her stomach reminded her that it had been several hours since lunch. Blythe removed the towel and replaced it

131

with a pale yellow silk robe that accentuated her dark eyes and hair. Like someone with an ulterior motive, she quietly opened the door of the dressing room, intending to rush out and swoop up her hair dryer before Micah could do more than blink his eyes.

But instead of seeing him seated in the chair by the window, where she'd assumed he would be, Blythe was somewhat disconcerted to see his long length comfortably sprawled on her bed, sleeping. His jacket, shoes, and tie had been thrown haphazardly toward the chair, and his shirt was open halfway down the front. One of his arms was bent behind his head, the other relaxed by his side.

She stood still; her gaze was riveted to his face and relaxed features. It had been a long time since she'd seen Micah sleeping. The last time had been the night before she ended their engagement.

She'd been spending the weekend with him at another of his hotels in southern Florida. That particular evening had been spent dining and dancing, and Blythe had felt like a princess, basking in the glow of Micah's attention like a rose unfolding to the gentle kiss of the morning sun. After they'd returned to the hotel, they'd made love. Later that night, she remembered awakening and pushing herself up on one elbow and simply staring at Micah, sleeping soundly, for a long time. In sleep, his features had been relaxed and softened. With a tentative finger she'd reached out and gently traced the line of his lips, lips that were capable of reducing her to a pliant, vulnerable woman in his arms. The happiness she'd felt at that moment had been overwhelming, bringing tears to her eyes.

Then Micah had awakened. His gaze had narrowed at the sparkling moistness in her eyes. No words had passed between them at that moment. It was as if he knew and understood the fragile balance of her emotions. He had reached out and caught her to him, his hands molding themselves to the slender lines of her body. The lovemaking that followed had been unlike anything they'd ever shared. An unbelievable sadness crept over Blythe as she remembered. It had also been the last time they'd made love.

An involuntary clenching of his fist broke the hypnotic spell that had woven itself around Blythe. She blinked as if to clear her thoughts, then walked silently toward the dresser and the hair dryer. Her hand reached out, but instead of feeling the laminated plastic in her grip, she found nothing but air. An arm of steel had snaked out and encircled her waist. Her feet left the floor, and she was pulled as effortlessly as a feather across muscled thighs to land in a yellow heap beside Micah.

"When a particular lady stands and stares at me with an intense look of longing on her face, I have to ask myself why," he murmured huskily. One arm was providing an exciting pillow for her neck while the other was lying across her bare thighs. Her robe had fallen open during her rather meteoric flight from floor to bed, and there was little but the silk and lace of her bra and matching panties to cover her from his probing gray eyes.

Blythe struggled to break the powerful merging of their gazes and tried to cover herself. It was a futile effort, so instead she glared at her assailant. "I was thinking how kind and human you looked asleep. After all, I'm only female and am allowed an occasional fanciful miscalculation," she snapped.

Micah abruptly shifted his body so that he was poised over her, one elbow supporting him. A heavy leg replaced his arm across her thighs, while his free hand went unerringly to the gentle swell of one breast.

"Don't you find me kind and human?" he persisted lightly. His forefinger began a delicate exploration of her swollen nipple beneath the lace, causing Blythe to take air into her lungs in tiny, biting gasps. From there his fingers inched their way to the indentations just above her collarbone. They circled and traced that tiny conclave, trailing across the delicate bone as well.

Slowly and deliberately, he worked his way over her pearly skin to the slender column of her neck. The tiny vein at the side was throbbing eagerly, and Micah smiled. Blythe saw triumph in that smile but was powerless to stop it. She watched as his head dipped forward, and she felt the velvety caress of his lips. Her lips parted. But his mouth didn't seek hers as she'd anticipated. His fingertip began to float across the surface of her lips, barely touching, creating an awareness more potent than if he had inflicted pain.

His leg across her thighs pressed harder against her, and Blythe—in spite of willing her body not to—felt the slow arching of her hips against a familiar warmth. "This is crazy," she whispered, her voice sounding faraway and distant.

"No," Micah sternly contradicted. "It's

right." He quickly slipped his hand beneath her back. After a moment or two Blythe felt the slight restriction of the bra loosened. The robe and the tiny straps were pushed off her shoulders, leaving her body open and bare to the fiery glow flowing from his eyes, a glow that was feeding the smoldering coals of passion within her. "It's not crazy," he said. "I've lain awake nights on end, thinking up ways to punish you for depriving me of the joy of looking at your body. Do you know that?"

Blythe was embarrassed and at the same time secretly thrilled. "I was not a possession," she reminded him in an attempt to regain even a small portion of her individuality. Micah had a way of absorbing a person. He'd done so before, but this time Blythe hoped she could be stronger.

A smile, tender and yet merciless, curved his lips. "You're my possession, Blythe Donaldson. You have been since that first night when I found you at a Christmas party." He bent his head to her breasts, letting it move back and forth as his lips worked with sheath-like suction that created an explosion of desire in her abdomen. The elastic edge of the bikini brief was lifted away from her body to make room for the thrust of his hand. Blythe closed her eyes against the drumming of blood throughout her body. The roar in her head was intensified by the closing of hard, firm fingers going to the center of her being. Pressing, stroking, pressing again . . . she was barely aware of lips leaving her breasts and being replaced by his hand. Each touch, each stroke of Micah's hands, each fiery caress of his tongue, was a flawless orchestration, the combination catapulting her into a breathless world where only he could breathe life into her, where only he could still the painful need wracking her body.

CHAPTER EIGHT

The only coherent thought in Blythe's mind was that if Micah didn't make love to her soon, she would die.

"I doubt it, honey," he said roughly. The timbre of his voice failed to dent the hazy mist of desire numbing Blythe to all but the indescribable need to feel him inside her. She wasn't at all aware that she'd actually spoken the words instead of thinking them.

What she *was* becoming aware of, however, was Micah's withdrawal. She opened drugged eyes and stared at him. "Micah?"

"Yes, Blythe?"

The way he said her name made her curiously reluctant to speak. "What's—I mean . . ."

"Why am I not making love to you?"

"Yes, that's it. Why aren't you making love to me instead of staring at me as if examining me beneath a microscope?"

"You're imagining things." He sat up, then raised his arms over his head and stretched. He turned and brushed a hand along her thigh. "Have you forgotten that we have a dinner date?"

"Dinner. Of course, how could I have forgotten?" She pulled at the yellow robe and covered herself, her mind reeling from his rebuff. Or was it a rebuff? Blythe asked herself. What kind of game was he playing? Strange, she mused ruefully, she should be lavishing thanks for not having completed his seduction. But she wasn't. In fact, the more she thought about his actions, the more unsettled she became. She couldn't even say he hadn't made love to her, for he had, though not with the actual merging of their bodies. He'd raised her to that last pinnacle of desire, only to leave her hanging, her needs unfulfilled.

Micah leaned over and put on his shoes, then got up and began dressing. "Will thirty minutes be enough time for you to get dressed?" he asked as politely as if addressing a casual acquaintance.

Blythe was tempted to tell him that she wasn't hungry, but pride wouldn't let her. "Thirty minutes will be fine. Why don't I meet you in the dining room?"

"Good idea. That will give me time to take care of a couple of things while I'm waiting." He suddenly leaned over her, a hand on either side of her face. "Thirty minutes is all, so don't be late." He dropped a quick kiss on her forehead and then left the room.

With movements uncharacteristically slow, Blythe rolled to the edge of the bed and stood. She brushed a trembling hand across her face, confusion and bewilderment starkly visible in each feature. She felt much the way she imagined a person would react after some wild and destructive storm had blasted its way through their life. Her body felt drained of energy, and it was an effort to place one foot before the other as she walked toward the dressing room.

Micah had wanted her—she was certain of that. Aside from the more obvious show of his arousal, she'd seen the same glow of passion in his eyes that had always been there when they'd made love. But something had held him back this time.

During the time it took her to dry her hair, apply her makeup, dress and regain a sense of normalcy, Blythe came to the conclusion that Micah's little erotic scene on the bed had been nothing more than a cold, calculated scheme. But why? The desire to humiliate each other had never been one of their habits. Well, she reasoned as she paused to stare at her reflection in the mirror, two could play Micah's little cat-and-mouse game as well as one, even if the rules were a bit hazy. With a defiant toss of her curly head, she reached for her small clutch purse, dropped her room key inside, and walked briskly toward the door.

The moment Blythe stepped from the elevator into the lobby, a bellboy came hurrying over to her. "Miss Donaldson?" he said politely. At Blythe's inquiring glance, he rushed on. "Mr. Caine said to tell you he would join you in the Crystal Room shortly. Seems there was a crisis with the chefs. If you'll just go down that corridor—" he nodded toward a door to the left of the front desk—"you won't have so far to walk. Both lounges, plus all the dining and ballrooms, have emergency exits opening into that hall. It's an extra safety feature the boss had built in when he bought this hotel."

After thanking the young man, Blythe crossed the lobby to the closed door. Upon opening it, she found herself in a long corridor with a tile floor. Obviously fireproof, she mused thoughtfully as she continued, pausing before each door until she found the one marked Crystal Room.

Blythe drew a deep steadying breath into her lungs as she grasped the knob and opened the door, with her head held high. When Micah had left her room less than an hour ago, she'd been like someone in a daze. Well, she sighed ruefully, the daze had passed. Now she wanted to show him how much in control she was, and to effectively squash any illusions he might be enjoying from having gotten her into his arms—and in her own bed no less—so easily. Those few minutes meant nothing to her, she kept telling herself, nothing at all.

And if she expected Micah to fall for that ridiculous line, her conscience hooted, then she should be committed!

The Crystal Room was one of the most beautiful Blythe had seen in this hotel or any other. As its name implied, large crystal chandeliers hung at intervals from the ceiling. The combined light from each multitiered fixture cast a willowy glow over the diners and the furnishings and was brilliantly reflected in the six tall, beveled mirrors hanging along the walls of the room. Large green plants sat beside dark, gleaming wood paneling, and there were touches of hand-rubbed brass throughout. Gleaming crystal, china, and silver settings on snowy damask graced each table.

Blythe knew immediately that she was going to enjoy her dinner. Even if the food was lousy, which she seriously doubted, the ambience of the Crystal Room would more than make up for such a small inconvenience.

"Ms. Donaldson?"

"Yes?" Blythe turned and smiled at a hovering waiter. His haughty air immediately set her nerves on edge; she disliked overbearing headwaiters. She also didn't like the idea of Micah giving her name to every damn one of his employees. It smacked of a certain possessiveness on his part that she didn't particularly care for.

"Mr. Caine left orders that you were to be shown to your table. He'll be joining you in just a few minutes. May I?" He gestured with one hand and nodded imperiously toward a table in a secluded corner of the dining room, virtually hidden by the artful placing of several large plants.

Blythe made no effort to move. She looked at the table for several seconds, ignoring the impatience she could feel seeping from the solemn-faced individual beside her. "Is that Mr. Caine's usual table?" She wasn't having the slightest difficulty imagining Micah sitting there with some other woman, and she was determined not to be so summarily placed by him or his snooty staff. Besides, she thought, the table, with its forest of greenery and its location in a corner by itself, reminded her of a royal bower.

"He changes from time to time. Occasionally he sits somewhere else, but generally he uses the corner table."

"What about the one by the window, is it reserved?"

"I don't believe so, but Mr.—"

Blythe patted the man's arm and smiled. "Then Mr. Caine will have to learn to be flexible—at least for this one time. I like that table better." She started forward and was some distance away before the startled waiter caught up with her.

This time he didn't extend his elbow. Instead, he grasped Blythe's arm and escorted

144

her to the table she'd chosen. "May I get you a drink while you're waiting?" he asked politely, but not quite masking his disapproval of her behavior.

"A glass of white wine." Blythe smiled. "You neglected to say what it is that's keeping Mr. Caine. Is he still having trouble with the chef?" She knew it wasn't proper to quiz the staff about Micah, but she was curious and the waiter was such a snob that she couldn't resist annoying him further.

"The chef has been sufficiently mollified. I believe the problem now has to do with one of the performers. Miss Kristi Barr, who is to begin a six-week engagement here in the Crystal Room, has arrived. She had some changes in mind, and Mr. Caine is discussing them with her. Excuse me, Miss Donaldson, while I get your wine."

It was all Blythe could do not to laugh at the frozen expression on his face and the stiff, unbending way he walked. She could just see him inflicting terror into the very souls of unsuspecting guests who dared to arrive at the gilded portals of his domain without reservations. It was quite evident from his manner that he considered himself—next to Micah, of course—the ruler of this tiny bejeweled kingdom.

Blythe watched the people in the room and had almost finished the glass of wine by the time she caught her first glimpse of Micah. He had paused just inside the double-doored entrance and was conferring with his trusted henchman. Blythe could almost feel her ears burn as she saw the sourpuss gesturing toward the secluded corner table, then shrug his shoulders. After a short conversation, Blythe watched Micah cross the room toward her, his long stride smooth and effortless.

As he pulled out a chair and sat down, he grinned at Blythe. "Must you be so hard on my staff? Renaldo is still in a state of shock that you demanded another table."

"Renaldo is a large pain in the rear," Blythe said shortly. "He acted as if you were Moses and your instructions were the Ten Commandments. I'm afraid I couldn't resist adding a few ripples to his life. He's too smug."

"True." Micah nodded with amusement. "But he does do a damn good job managing this room." Suddenly, Renaldo and his managerial abilities were forgotten as he let his gaze slowly ease over Blythe's slim neck and shoulders, which were bare except for the tiny straps of the pale green dress she was wearing. In his mind's eye he saw her as he'd left her only an hour or so ago, lying on her bed, her small exquisite body smoldering with desire. The pink nipples cresting her breasts had been hard, and her breasts had been swollen with passion. He should have taken her then, he kept telling himself, should have taken her and been done with it. But he loved her. And because of that he wanted their lovemaking to be shared, not something he'd demanded or forced on her. Blythe had to want him as intensely as he wanted her. Still, he was afraid the longer he waited, the more barriers Blythe would erect between them.

"I'm sorry to have kept you waiting," he murmured huskily, reaching out to gently caress her palm, his touch causing Blythe to want to jerk her hand away and hide it beneath the table. His touch was maddening, she told herself.

"Were you able to—satisfy Miss Barr?"

It was a cheap shot. Blythe instantly criticized herself, but at that precise moment she needed all the insulation possible against Micah's charm.

"She has a unique way of negotiating. I'm

looking forward to her engagement here," he replied unruffled. He couldn't believe it. His little brown-eyed vixen was jealous. He struggled to keep the pleasure from showing in his face. Jealousy from Blythe was something he hadn't hoped to see so soon. "If you like, I'll introduce you to her."

"Of course." Blythe smiled, though she was sure her cheeks would crack with the effort. "I'd love to meet her." In a pig's eye, she silently scoffed. She'd seen Kristi Barr's type before. She'd probably be running to Micah with a different problem every day. "Have you heard anything more from the police about the break-ins?"

Micah frowned. "Nothing. I checked with Lieutenant Harris about thirty minutes ago. He thinks it was a prankster. But prankster or not, I can't tolerate something like that happening in one of my hotels. It places my guests in possible danger and makes my security people look incompetent."

Blythe smiled, amused by the scowling man sitting next to her. "Since I was the only guest involved, yours and the reputation of your security people shall remain unblemished. Isn't that extremely kind of me?" she teased.

"Oh my, yes." Micah smiled lazily, and

Blythe could feel the awful wrenching in the pit of her stomach as the lambent gleam in his gray-blue eyes fused with hers. "We'll make a deal. My personal protection against further intruders for your silence. Deal?"

"Just how personal will your protection be?" She barely murmured the words as she felt his warm fingers against the side of her throat. *Dear Lord.* He was barely touching her, but he was making love to her in a room full of people as surely as if he'd undressed her and was possessing her naked body.

"More personal than you can ever imagine," Micah replied huskily, letting his fingers trail down to the fragile indentation of her collarbone. "Nothing jarring or displeasing, I assure you. One morning or evening or noon, you'll suddenly realize that having my protection has become such a vital part of your existence that you won't want to do without it."

"If I didn't know you better, I'd say you were bragging."

"As you said, you know me better. I never brag. Am I frightening you?"

"I'm a big girl, Micah."

He leaned back in his chair, his elbows resting on the arms of his chair, while the tips of his fingers came together and formed an arch against his lips. "So you are," he murmured, an inexplicable expression softening his features. "So you are."

CHAPTER NINE

All through dinner, Blythe found herself being both delightfully entertained by Micah and involved in a subtle conversation in which mere words had nothing at all to do with the true meaning being conveyed.

By the time dessert arrived, she could almost feel her head spinning. Micah was looking enormously pleased with himself.

"Did you say Stephen was due to arrive in a day or two?" When she saw his facial muscles tighten at the mention of his brother's name, Blythe knew a small moment of victory.

"Anytime now."

"It'll be nice seeing him again," Blythe remarked pleasantly, ignoring Micah's grim expression. "He always seemed to keep some kind of mischief going."

"Didn't he," Micah muttered darkly. "Would you care for something else?"

"Nothing, thank you. The food was delicious, but I refuse to pander to the egotistical Renaldo by telling him so."

"Shall I do it for you?" Micah grinned teasingly.

"Don't you dare."

"You've turned into something of a scrapper in the past two years, haven't you?"

"I suppose I have," Blythe concurred. She regarded him levelly, her gaze unflinching. "I even enjoy a good fight these days, figuratively speaking of course, and I definitely do not care to be manipulated by others."

"That's good." Micah responded without the slightest show of concern in his voice. "Because I have an intense dislike of weak opponents."

Blythe raised the wineglass to her lips. "Oh? Have we agreed to outright war?" she asked over the rim.

"We've been trading insults like two enemy countries since the day you walked out on me," Micah reminded her.

"Evening."

"I beg your pardon?"

"It was evening when I walked out on you."

"I'm surprised you remember."

"Oh, I remember. It was on a Monday evening at eight-forty-seven."

Micah leaned forward. The movement brought him uncomfortably close to Blythe. At that moment she'd much rather have had him sitting across the table from her than to her right. "And you want me to believe that you no longer care for me?" His voice was husky, vibrant. "If you're as indifferent as you try to appear, then why is the date and the hour of my supposed infidelity so easy for you to remember?"

"Don't gloat, Micah," Blythe said evenly. "It doesn't become you. But if you must have an answer"—she shrugged resignedly—"I also remember the times and dates of my last two visits to the dentist. Does that shed some light on my dying passion for you?"

"God, but you are a mean-hearted woman." Micah scowled as he dropped back into his chair. "I thought you had decided I wasn't unfaithful to you?"

"How did that subject get into our conversation?" Blythe looked surprised.

"The not-so-subtle way you pointed out

your excellent memory for time and dates where painful experiences were had."

"Oh."

"Just 'Oh'?" he asked sourly.

"What else would you like me to say?"

"That you've finally gotten over that damn childish notion that I was sleeping with other women, for one thing."

"Childish?" Blythe repeated in amazement.

"Damn right. Childish, stupid, ridiculous— call it what you will, it all adds up to the same thing. You jumped to the wrong conclusion, but you're too damn stubborn to admit it. Consequently, you've put us both through all kinds of hell rather than admit you were wrong. You were even silly enough to rush out and marry that two-bit Casanova Talbot Ames."

"You leave Talbot out of this," Blythe retorted. "And just to set the record straight, let's look at a few things regarding *your* behavior, shall we?"

"Be my guest." Micah waved one large hand magnanimously. "However, don't you think it would be less embarrassing if we continued this conversation somewhere else?"

"Why?" Blythe thrust out her small chin mulishly, determined not to give an inch.

"Because people are beginning to stare at us," she was told in a clipped voice. "I think my apartment would give us ample freedom, don't you?"

"Too much," Blythe told him without blinking as she rose to her feet. "We'll take a walk along the beach. We can have just as much freedom there."

"You act like I'm going to get you drunk and seduce you," Micah grumbled as he held her chair for her, then grasped her elbow and escorted her from the room.

"How can you sound so innocent when I know that's exactly what's on your mind? I also haven't forgotten how very persuasive you can be. In fact"—she stared up at him, trying for a stern look but failing miserably—"it hasn't been that long since I witnessed those same powers of persuasion at work—on me."

"At least I haven't lost my touch." Micah chuckled without the slightest trace of repentance.

"No," Blythe admitted ruefully, "you haven't lost a darn thing." She paused at the edge of the grass next to the glistening white

155

sand and removed her shoes, her hand cling-
ing to Micah's arm for balance.

"Correction, sweetheart," his husky voice
reminded her mockingly as he stood patiently, "I lost you."

"Not because you were lacking as a lover,"
Blythe rather crisply reminded him. "I just
never quite recovered from seeing you with-
stand that woman's advances so admirably.
You didn't raise one lousy finger in protest."

"And for that you were willing to consign
my soul to hell and further humiliate me by
marrying Ames?" Micah asked incredulously.

"Was I supposed to applaud you? Was there
some law that said I was obliged to stand
around like a fool while you allowed your
body to be pawed by any woman who happened to take a fancy to you?"

"You make it sound like I was enjoying that
blonde's attentions," Micah tried to defend
himself.

"You were." Blythe sighed. "The expression
on your face was—captivated."

"I can't even remember what she looked
like, so I seriously doubt I was lost in a world
of sexual delight as you seem to think I was."
Micah responded with such masculine assur-
ance that Blythe was tempted to find a club

156

and smack him across his conceited head. "What you don't seem to understand, honey, is that in my business, I come in contact with as many women as men. I don't mean to sound like a heel"—he shrugged—"but it doesn't mean anything to me when women let me know subtly or otherwise that they're interested in me."

"How noble. But it wasn't the contact that bothered me," Blythe answered. "It was the cordial way you seemed to make yourself available to her. What would you have thought if you'd walked into a room and found me in the same situation with a man? Would you have simply walked over and shaken the man's hand?"

"How the hell should I know?" Micah exclaimed.

"Don't be an evasive ass," Blythe said scornfully. "Give me an answer."

"All right." He sighed roughly. "I probably would have knocked the guy's head off. Does that satisfy you?" The moon was bright, its light bathing the grounds and the beach in a soft, ethereal glow. Micah could see the satisfaction on Blythe's face.

"Some," she admitted. "But I think what

I'm beginning to really discover is how differently we regard life."

"What's that supposed to mean?" Micah glared at her.

"Oh, a casual pat on a fanny here, a bit of smooching there. A few stolen kisses—maybe even a night together—" She looked up at Micah and smiled. "You do get my drift?"

"Sure." He nodded. "You've just described a part of my life before I met you. Along with a freedom to do and enjoy certain things, wealth also brings undesirable factions into one's life—mainly parasites in the form of human beings. You'd be surprised how many people there are who are eager to share my money with me. I've had women do a hell of a lot more than crawl naked into my bed in order to try and get my attention. At least the blonde you seem so determined to hate wasn't after a single thing from me." He grinned. "She was about the most free-spirited individual I've ever run into, but she wasn't interested in a single penny of my money."

"But don't you see?" Blythe said earnestly. "When you talk of the different escapades in your life, there's a special kind of lilt in your voice that makes me wonder how you think you can change. The women, the booze, the play-all-night, sleep-all-day routine. You love it."

"Grow up, honey. I didn't pat any fannies or kiss anybody while we were engaged," he immediately replied. "I didn't want to. And I damn sure didn't take another woman to my bed. As for enjoying my lifestyle, I suppose I do—up to a point. But what's wrong with that? I've worked damn hard for everything I have, Blythe. It hasn't been handed to me by adoring relatives."

"That's not fair," she cried. "Carrie and Amanda are the only family I have. They love me. Naturally they want to do things for me."

"Of course," Micah nodded. "And that's the way it should be. But while you've been accepting all that love from them over the years, it's caused your outlook on life to become rather narrow."

Blythe planted her feet in the sand, thrust her fists on her hips, and angrily regarded him. "Now you listen just a da—"

"No, you listen," Micah interrupted with equal force. He too had swung around, his stance not as menacing as Blythe's, but alert nonetheless. "I can't believe you're so narrow-minded that you let what you think my past was like keep us from having a future."

"Explain, please," Blythe said haughtily.

"If you insist," Micah snapped. "Frankly, I think there's more to it than your being afraid you can't trust me. Hasn't it ever occurred to you that in addition to sleeping with at least a different woman every night, I'm also some sort of lowlife as well?" Micah challenged. "Can you honestly say the thought hasn't crossed your mind that I'm probably involved with all types of unsavory people who deal in everything from prostitution to gambling and drugs?"

Even in the moonlight the flush of embarrassment that was quick to sweep over Blythe's face was remarkably clear. "I suppose I could deny any such thoughts."

"You could."

"But you know it would be pointless, don't you?"

"Certainly."

Blythe turned and stared out at the bay, warring with her own thoughts at the moment. For the past two years she'd been so busy blaming Micah, she had never stopped to realize how much of an exacting wretch she had been. If she were honest with herself

160

and with him, she would have to admit that the question of whether Micah was involved in some sort of illegal activity had crossed her mind.

His lifestyle had been and still was different from hers, she admitted. Different and exciting. He had grown accustomed to rubbing shoulders with celebrities and all sorts of important people during the course of a month, a week—even a day. Consequently, he had unwittingly developed a certain veneer that kept the real face of Micah Caine hidden from the public eye.

Yet Blythe knew that he had been himself with her. She'd known him in moments of unbelievable tenderness and gentleness as well as in moments of intense anger. They had laughed together and loved together. But in the end, the laughter and the loving hadn't been a strong enough bond to bridge the differences in their backgrounds.

"It's rather ironic that we're having this particular conversation this evening, at this point in our life," she muttered huskily.

"Why is that?" Micah asked. He dropped an arm across her shoulders and caught her close to his side, then urged her on along the beach.

Blythe welcomed the feel of his body

pressed against hers. Even the familiar scent of him brought with it a fleeting sense of completeness that momentarily centered itself in her thoughts, then just as quickly disappeared, as elusive as a shadowy mist. "Because I spent the greater part of this afternoon convincing myself that I'd finally sorted out all my problems where you were concerned. It's also rather like having the horse before the cart. We're discussing our differences almost two years after those same differences broke up our engagement."

"Foolish woman," Micah murmured, his lips brushing against her hair. "Haven't you learned by now that there are times when sane, logical reasoning can be frustrating as hell?"

She sighed forlornly. "Right now I'm more confused than ever. Do you do it deliberately?"

"Do what?" Micah gently asked.

"Concentrate on keeping me confused," Blythe said bluntly.

"I'm afraid, sweetheart, the confusion is more in your own mind than anywhere else. In fact, this entire situation arose from your inability to stop and really look at the situation. Rather than thinking, you reacted, and

162

because of that we lost two years of our lives that could have been very beautiful."

"That's what *you* say," Blythe murmured defensively. "But we're still very different people, with two distinct personalities, two totally opposite points of view. And we've even added a couple of things in two years. You think I'm a spoiled brat. I think you're a wealthy playboy with a very liberal outlook on sex and life in general."

Micah regarded her through narrowed lids, his mouth a grim slash. "Why do I get the feeling that in that strange, mixed-up way of yours, you've almost exonerated me of having been unfaithful to you, and now you're throwing up this new and ridiculous barrier between us of my wealth, my lack of background, and my promiscuity. I'm beginning to wonder what there was in the beginning that attracted you to me. I sure as hell haven't changed. What are you really afraid of, Blythe?"

"Me—afraid?"

"You, sweetheart, and don't try to deny it. You love me, I love you. I don't think either of us will argue that point. Yet you seem incapable of allowing us to share our lives together. There has to be a reason for your strange behavior, and I won't stop until I find out what it is."

Blythe wanted to tell him that he was being foolish, but deep inside she knew he had spoken the truth. For there were doubts in her mind, in her heart. In a sense she was frightened of trying to make a life with Micah. Perhaps seeing him two years ago with another woman had sparked a chain of events that had kept them apart, but even now Blythe was afraid the difference in their thinking and their lifestyles would keep them from having a happy, healthy relationship, much less a happy marriage. Opposites were supposed to attract, she told herself dejectedly, but in her and Micah's case, the differences were too vast, the price too high.

Before, she had been a young, easily impressed girl. Since that time, she'd matured into a woman, a woman unimpressed with the glamour and glitter of a life that she knew she would have difficulty accepting. She also wanted the man in her life to be hers alone. She would never share him with other women.

CHAPTER TEN

Blythe awakened the next morning with a throbbing headache, no doubt the result of her lack of sleep. It had been almost daylight before she'd gotten any rest because she tossed and turned, her thoughts totally absorbed in Micah.

As she stared at the ceiling, it occurred to Blythe that for all her hours of mental gyrations, she might just as well have saved herself the time and trouble. There was no easy solution to her problem with Micah. If anything, things were more complicated; her original argument with him had been pushed into the background by two or three new problems.

Rather than start off the day by viewing her

dilemma as depressing and beyond saving, Blythe threw back the covers and swung her feet to the floor. Being a pessimist had never appealed to her. But that seemed to be what she had become in the last few days, she told herself. A droopy-lipped, sad-eyed pessimist. She hurried to the bathroom, where she reached inside the shower and adjusted the water. As she slipped out of her gown, she glanced at her reflection in the mirror above the dressing table. Perhaps Micah was right after all, she told herself. Perhaps she was spoiled. Her life, thanks to her aunts, had been almost perfect. They'd cushioned the hurt of losing her parents and had continued protecting and encouraging her ever since.

The only jarring note in her rosy world had been when she thought Micah had been unfaithful to her. And though they had tried, there was nothing the aunts had been able to do to prevent the pain she'd suffered.

But now? a tiny voice asked. Why was she suddenly dredging up all these other reasons why she and Micah couldn't possibly have a life together? What was she really afraid of?

It was the same question Micah had asked her the evening before, Blythe realized as she stepped into the shower and turned her face up to the water. The problem was, after a night of searching, she still didn't have an answer.

Forty-five minutes later, Blythe entered the dining room and was shown to a table. Without looking at the menu, she gave her order of scrambled eggs, bacon, toast, and coffee to the attractive waitress, then settled back into her chair and began reading the newspaper she'd bought in the lobby.

She'd worked her way through to the fourth page when an item tucked away on an inside corner caught her attention. Blythe unconsciously brought the paper closer as she read the account of Allen Johnson, an accountant who had been killed by a hit-and-run driver. The last few sentences of the article brought a startled gasp from Blythe. Mr. Johnson had been scheduled to testify on the government's behalf in a fraud case. The corporation where he'd previously been employed and which was also considered a giant in the corporate world was accused of systematically bilking the government out of millions of dollars over the last few years.

According to the story, Allen Johnson had headed up the accounting department for the corporation until four months ago. Without really coming out and saying it, the article gave the distinct impression that more than mere coincidence surrounded the accountant's death.

"That's terrible," Blythe muttered, her expression thoughtful as she continued to stare at the newspaper.

"What's so terrible?" a deep voice asked close to her ear the same moment a pair of lips brushed the angle of her jaw.

"Micah!" Blythe murmured warningly, her face turning an attractive pink at his open display of affection. She watched him move to the chair to her right, then glanced quickly around to see if they really were the center of attention that she imagined them to be.

"See?" Micah teased, his gaze sweeping possessively over her. "Not a single soul saw us. Feel better?"

"Yes. I don't normally neck in a public restaurant." Blythe tried to sound stern.

"Perhaps you should. You'd be surprised what can happen when you break away from your established routine."

Blythe pointed with one long, pink-tipped finger to the article she'd been reading. "Mmm. Apparently, Mr. Johnson was a believer in your philosophy. At any rate, it appears he certainly tried something a little different. The problem is, it got him killed."

Micah threw her a puzzled look and reached for the paper. After scanning the account of Allen Johnson's death, he stared curiously at Blythe. "Have I missed something? I fail to see how suggesting that you unbend a little can possibly be tied in with this poor guy's death."

"Didn't my aunts tell you about seeing a man get run down by a hit-and-run driver while they were on one of their contest-related jaunts?"

"No. When was this?"

"A few days before we came here," Blythe told him, then explained in detail what had happened. "That's what made this vacation seem like the perfect solution to the problem," she added. "I was really beginning to worry about them."

"Did the police question them?"

"According to Carrie and Amanda, the investigating officers treated the accident as a simple hit-and-run, even though the aunts were quick to tell them that they thought it was deliberate. They haven't been contacted since, though the police know they're here.

The fact that their 'nice gentleman' was to be a government witness makes me uneasy."

"I have a couple of friends who happen to be connected with law enforcement. I'll contact them and see if there's been any break in the case. Will that make you feel better?"

Blythe smiled. "Much better, thank you. But please don't mention anything about the accident to my aunts. Since they haven't spoken of it, I can only assume they're trying to put it out of their minds. Though there is one thing."

"What's that?"

"Do you suppose their suite being broken into had anything to do with Allen Johnson's death?" Blythe asked.

Micah absently stirred the cup of coffee he'd just poured. A thoughtful twist pulled at his mouth. "I don't see how. Besides, your room was ransacked as well, and you were nowhere near the accident."

"I suppose you're right." She sighed.

"Why don't we put all cloak-and-dagger thoughts from our minds for today and concentrate on something far more enjoyable?" he suggested.

Blythe regarded him suspiciously. "Such as?"

"My first choice would be the two of us spending the day in bed making love—preferably in some secluded spot where there's no phone."

"My, you're resourceful early in the morning." Blythe nodded with a straight face. "What's your second choice? With your imagination, I know there has to be another idea."

Micah tipped his head forward a fraction. "Your flattery overwhelms me, Ms. Donaldson," he remarked facetiously. "What would you say to a well-stocked picnic basket, a blanket, a secluded cove, and a nice chilled bottle of wine?"

"You're incorrigible," Blythe accused. "You know I adore picnics."

"Of course." Micah smiled unashamedly. "That's all part of my plan to get you back. I intend to take advantage of every weakness you possess."

"You're despicable."

He nodded. "Correct. I do have one redeeming quality, though."

"Name it."

"I love you."

Blythe wanted to look away from the love in his gray-blue eyes, but for the life of her, she couldn't. It was as if the force of his feelings were a tangible thing, encircling her, forcing her to acknowledge its presence.

"You're doing it again," she said breathlessly.

"Doing what, honey?"

"Trying to confuse me."

"Correction, sweetheart," Micah said with a laugh. "You don't need my help with that, you do it all on your own. If having to accept that I wasn't unfaithful to you and that I love you is confusing, that's too bad. I offer no apology, and I certainly won't fade quietly into the woodwork."

The thought of Micah being meek and submissive brought a smile to Blythe's face in spite of the emotional turmoil within her at the moment. "You really aren't going to make any of this easy for me, are you?"

"Tell me something, Blythe," Micah said after quietly regarding her for a moment. "Exactly what do you mean by 'any of this'?"

It was an odd question, and Blythe looked confused. "This," she repeated for lack of a better word as she lifted her hands in indecision. "My feelings, this peculiar relationship we've found ourselves in. It's difficult to put a name to it."

"Why not call it by its real name?" he quietly suggested.

"Which is?"

"Love. Our love for each other. Why is it so difficult for you to say the words?"

"Because I'm not sure it really is love, at least for me," she said honestly. "In fact, I've begun to wonder if it ever really was." Micah's look of incredulity was so extreme that Blythe found herself chuckling softly.

"And if you believe that, then I have some land to sell you just east of here," he retorted sharply. "You love me now just as you loved me two years ago. Your only problem is your incredible ego. With your crazy logic, you think the best way to punish me is to suddenly decide what you feel for me is nothing but friendship."

During this cryptic little speech, Blythe felt herself undergo a tremendous change. One moment she was reasonably happy and content; the next, she could feel her face beginning to burn with anger. "Are you finished?"

"For the moment," Micah said, his square chin thrust forward belligerently.

"Good." Blythe pushed back her chair and rose to her feet. "When my breakfast arrives, will you please tell the waitress that due to the

173

unwelcome attentions of a singleminded boor, I've lost my appetite." She turned on her heel and swept from the room angrily, her chin held high.

In her room, Blythe slammed the door shut, then began pacing. *Damn!* It simply wasn't fair. This was supposed to be a vacation, not an incarceration. Yet about the only way she could be sure of not running into Micah was to stay in her room.

Her aunts had deserted her. Lying in the sun was out of the question—with his network of spies at work, Micah would know her whereabouts in no time. A leisurely stroll through the grounds would produce the same result as sunbathing. There was also a limit to the number of drives one could take, especially when it was a matter of having to instead of really wanting to go sightseeing.

She brought her restless pacing to a halt by the window. The smarting sensation of tears stung her eyes. Micah's words had hit a nerve. In fact, everything about him lately seemed to have directly caused or brought about some upheaval in her life. And, she breathed raggedly, it so happened that just about every damn reference he made to their relationship had merit. She *did* love him, she told herself grimly as she stared unseeingly toward the beach, but that was a fact that she hadn't the slightest desire to share with him. She'd become an expert at playing down her feelings where he was concerned.

Blythe shook her head in dismay when she remembered how innocently she'd accepted Micah in the halcyon days of their early idyllic romance. "Rose-colored glasses" would be putting it mildly—she must have been totally blind.

A commanding knock on the door broke the painfully reflective spell. Blythe walked across the room. "Who is it?" she asked, her hand poised above the knob. Her look through the peephole revealed a cart with several covered dishes.

"Room service."

"Well, at least the fink had the decency to send me some food," she murmured. She released the chain and opened the door.

"I hope you're hungry, sweetheart," Micah said easily. He pushed the loaded cart past an open-mouthed Blythe, not stopping until he reached the table before the window. "Is French toast still one of your favorites?" he asked as he snapped a snowy white cloth into place, followed by china and flatwear. A steaming cup of coffee was placed in the center of the table. Satisfied that all was in order, he turned to a flinty-eyed Blythe. "Shall we eat?"

CHAPTER ELEVEN

She could order him from the room, Blythe told herself as she favored Micah with a malevolent glare. She could even rush over and start flinging food to the floor. Instead, she calmly walked over to the table, sat down, flicked the napkin across her thighs, and began serving her plate.

"May I join you?" Micah asked with suspicious humbleness.

"If you must." Blythe shrugged indifferently.

Several moments went by without a word passing between them, moments during which Blythe was racking her brain to come up with some irritating remark for her breakfast companion.

"It's good to see that our little difference of opinion hasn't put you off food," the constant pain in her side smartly quipped, a smug expression on his face.

"Just because you're an ass and have dedicated yourself to perfecting the appropriate personality for such a being, I can't see that it would benefit me in the least to starve myself."

"Cute, Blythe. Real cute."

"Thank you, Micah." She smiled grimly before she took a sip of coffee. "If you'll let me know your plans for the day, I promise to stay as far away as possible."

"Ah." Micah grinned. "If I were to do something as accommodating as that, then it wouldn't possibly fit in with my image as an ass, would it? No"—he shook his dark blond head—"I'm afraid not, Blythe. I'd much rather operate under the element of surprise."

"That's understandable," she muttered darkly, and then lapsed into another stony silence.

To add insult to injury, Micah didn't seem the least bit distressed by her mood. He picked up the newspaper he'd brought along and began to read it. After what seemed like an interminable length of time of being ignored, Blythe jumped up and flounced into the dressing room. With careless disregard for their fragility, she scooped up several pieces of lingerie and a blouse, dumped them into the sink, and turned on the faucet.

Suddenly, Micah materialized beside her and leaned against the counter. "We have excellent valet and maid service here at the hotel. Have you tried either of them?"

"No."

"Perhaps you will later," he replied unruffled. "By the way, can you be ready by eleven o'clock?"

"Ready for what?" Blythe asked tersely.

"Our picnic. Remember?"

"I'll be busy at eleven."

"I know, love. You'll be busy with me."

"I am not going on a picnic with you, Micah," Blythe enunciated carefully and precisely. "Understand?"

"Of course, sweetheart," he answered without a great deal of conviction. He leaned forward at the same moment that his hand caught her chin and forced her to look up at him. But instead of having to deal with words,

Blythe found herself attempting to evade his mouth.

"I don't want to kiss you any more than I want to go on a picnic with you," she said from between clenched teeth.

"I can't believe there's so much hostility in such a little thing." Micah hooked his other arm around Blythe's waist and almost lifted her off her feet as he turned her toward his body. The blouse she'd been clutching dropped with a generous splash into the sink.

"Doesn't the word *no* mean anything to you?" Blythe demanded as haughtily as her position allowed. It was very difficult to keep her grievances against Micah foremost in her mind when his large, powerful body was pressed so intimately against her own, she grudgingly admitted. If only she wouldn't respond so quickly to him, but she did—every time he took her into his arms.

"That word isn't in my vocabulary," Micah murmured huskily. "I refuse to allow it to be spoken anywhere near me. Especially when I'm holding you in my arms and remembering what it was like making love to you." His breath was warm and it smelled of coffee as he eased his lips back and forth lightly across her mouth. His hand released her chin and dipped down across her neck to the inviting fullness of her breasts. When he touched the betraying thrust of first one nipple and then the other, he shook his head at Blythe and heaved a sigh filled with resignation and contentment. "How long, Blythe? How damn long do you plan on continuing this farce? How long do you plan on punishing me for something you know damn well I'm not guilty of?"

"Punishment, Micah? If that's what it is, then it must be a two-edged sword. I haven't enjoyed it any more than you." Later, Blythe knew she would be forced to examine his words. For somewhere in the nether regions of her mind, she'd begun to ask herself that same question. Painting Micah as the villain in her mind—at first—had been so easy, and she'd clung to that opinion with a singlemindedness that was unusual even for her. But lately she couldn't help but wonder if she'd been wrong, if she'd convicted him without a fair trial. Had she been wrong all this time?

But enough introspection, she thought dreamily. At the moment all she was interested in was emerging unscathed—at least outwardly—from this latest bout with Micah, if such a thing were possible. From the way his hands were confidently warming their way over her back and hips, though, she could almost swear she wouldn't be the winner.

His mouth descended onto Blythe's, forceful and demanding as it stormed the iciness of her resolve and shattered her determination. His tongue blazed a bold yet gentle entrance into the velvet darkness of her mouth, engaging her tongue in an artful and erotic dance that brought their bodies instinctively closer. A blending of emotions and desires flamed and peaked into fires that were ready to burst out of control.

Micah suddenly raised his head, his eyes smoldering with passion, his breathing raspy and labored. "I think the moment has come to lay the past to rest, honey." One large hand took quiet possession of her nape, leaving Blythe, as always, a little in awe of how gentle this large man's touch could be.

It was a statement to which no reply was necessary. Even if she'd had days or weeks to consider the words, she knew in her heart the answer would be the same. It *was* time to put the past to rest. She'd let it eat away at her for almost two years, clouding her vision in every possible way where Micah was concerned. It had warped her thinking and had left her emotionally unfit for any kind of future relationship.

When her hand was caught up by his larger one and she felt herself being urged from the dressing room, Blythe made no effort to break away. It felt right. There was no sense of panic in her as they walked toward the bed, no embarrassment.

This was the first man who had ever made love to her. He'd been the first to awaken her body and her senses, the first to carry her to that magic summit where two incredibly vulnerable entities had merged as one and forged a bond of indescribable beauty.

The bed became a brilliant backdrop of sunny yellow, broken only by the slowly undulating shadows of the tall plant beside the window, its long leaves kept in gentle motion by the morning breeze coming in off the ocean.

"Yellow becomes you," Micah said in a husky timbre that Blythe had heard often in the past. He released his hold on her hand, then brought his fingers up to her shoulder to insinuate themselves beneath the tiny straps of the top she was wearing.

"Thank you," Blythe murmured, her gaze riveted to the swirling storm of passion growing in his eyes. *Color be damned*, she thought dazedly, she didn't care if yellow made her look like a fish. All she wanted—no, she argued with herself, that wasn't the way it was at all—what she *needed* was Micah's arms around her. She needed to be surrounded by him, with the feel, the scent, and the taste of him permeating her senses. He was the catharsis she needed to rid herself of two years of hurt, of disappointment and anger at him for having failed her.

Blythe closed her eyes as Micah's hands drew the blouse over her head and let it fall to the floor. She sucked in her breath as the edges of his thumbs scraped against the sides of her breasts on their way to the waistband of her shorts. His hands seemed to be in ten different places at once, removing bits and pieces of clothing, his touch as firm and reassuring as she remembered it to be.

Micah stared at Blythe through narrowed lids that closed in precious agony from time to time as wave after wave of desire slammed through his veins. The way she reacted as he slowly revealed her body was more potent than any aphrodisiac made by man or nature.

His lungs filled with the breath of anticipation as his softly probing fingers slipped between her thighs and pressed against the dusky, shadowy essence of her desire. Her arousal, though manifested in an entirely different way, was just as great as his own.

Blythe heard a soft moan shoot from her throat as her head dropped back and her eyes closed at the touch of sure fingers against the inner softness of her thighs. Her fingers clutched Micah's shoulders for support. For one incredible moment, she couldn't decide which was worse, the pain she'd suffered during the last two years or the unbelievable agony he was putting her through at the moment.

"Undress me, Blythe," Micah whispered. "Put your hands on me—all over me. Touch me like I'm touching you. Love me the way you once did."

His clothes were disposed of swiftly. When he stood naked before her with his tan, fit body full of energy and life, Blythe knew a quiet moment of unequaled joy. Slowly, deliberately, Blythe's hands closed about him, first on his head, molding her fingers to the shape of his skull. Then her fingers wove like a sorcerer's touch through the dark blond thickness of his hair. His face was next, and she explored his rugged profile, then his neck, his chest, the tautness of his waist and hips, and the muscled firmness of his buttocks and thighs.

The whispery movement of her fingertips became an artist's paintbrush, delineating a perfect sketch of the gorgeous male body before her, then filling in substance and shape with the touch of her lips and the erotic tracings of her tongue against his warm skin.

With roughness that bespoke his impatience, Micah's hands went to Blythe's forearms and lifted her until her face was level with his. His arms slipped into place around her and cradled her upper body to him like a second skin while his thighs framed her legs.

"You are so beautiful, sweetheart." He sounded drugged, and his eyes were luminous pools that fairly glowed as he stared at her. "Funny," he grinned, his attention straying to the tops of her breasts pressed against his chest. "I never really thought of the morning as being a sexy time of day." He leaned his head forward until his forehead was resting against her chest, and he let the tip of his moist tongue trace lazy patterns around the tips of her breasts.

"How could you have been so remiss all this time?" Blythe quipped innocently. Without warning, she leaned forward and bit him sharply on the shoulder.

"Ouch!" Micah yelled. "That hurt, you little vixen."

"Sue me." Blythe was undaunted.

"Why should I sue you," Micah asked silkily, "when I have you naked in my arms? There are much more delightful forms of revenge." With a slow, unhurried effort, he lowered her feet to the floor, rubbing her body against his as he did. His large hands splayed over the rounded firmness of her buttocks and squeezed. "Such as—seeing if you're still ticklish."

"Don't you dare!" Blythe squealed, laughing as his fingertips ran in a feathery tattoo along her skin. Her squirming to gain release from her captor and his efforts to thwart her endeavors ended with them falling onto the bed in a laughing, squirming tangle of arms and legs.

"Oh, but I must," Micah countered, easily controlling her movements by slipping his heavy legs on either side of hers and lying almost fully on top of her with his weight supported by his elbows. "I'll have you know that you've insulted me and inflicted bodily harm without the slightest regard for my feelings. I want my revenge."

Suddenly, Blythe sobered. Her gaze met and held Micah's laughing one. "Believe me, Micah, revenge brings a wealth of unhappiness."

Her quiet words removed the smile from Micah's lips. He framed her face with his hands and gazed down at her. "Are you unhappy at this particular moment?"

An easy, mischievous grin slowly spread over her face. She looked down at as much of his naked chest and stomach as she could see and at her own body. "In view of the situation, don't you think that's rather a silly question?"

"Not necessarily," Micah replied. "Can you honestly say you didn't have some idea of revenge in mind when you decided to come to bed with me?"

"Yes," she said after a thoughtful pause. "I suppose I was thinking of revenge, though for the life of me, I can't figure out exactly how us making love was supposed to have an adverse affect on you." She lifted one shoulder. "Unless some wild, fleeting thought whizzed through my mind that it would cause you pain to know what you'd given up so easily. Does that make sense? But how were you able to tell what I was thinking?"

Micah chuckled, the sound of it causing a reverberation deep in his chest that wasn't unpleasant in the least. "Of course it makes sense. It's a very human reaction. It's also a very egotistical one. And I knew what you were thinking because I've always been able to read your thoughts, for the most part. It's like that with some people."

The only word Blythe heard, however, was *egotistical.* "Move your stinking carcass off me," she demanded. "Egotistical, indeed! I'll make you think egotistical."

CHAPTER TWELVE

"Of all the unfavorable traits you've supposedly found in me, stupidity is not among them. Twelve sticks of dynamite couldn't blow me off this bed," Micah said with conviction. "And just to set the record straight, what I said wasn't necessarily aimed at you."

"Oh?" Blythe raised her head and pretended to look around the room. "I didn't know there was anyone else in here with us."

Micah's heavy hands gripped her shoulders and he gave her a quick shake, his gray eyes blazing, leaving her with little doubt of his irritation. "What I meant was that, human nature being what it is, it wasn't uncommon for you to want me to feel regret at having lost you. I experienced something similar when you married Talbot. It became an obsession with me, hoping that, when the two of you made love, you'd find him so inadequate that it would leave you unfulfilled and yearning for me."

Blythe looked away from the piercing intensity of his gaze, a little embarrassed that he'd so accurately described the real relationship that had existed between her and Talbot. Having Micah know just how bad her marriage had been would be humiliating.

"I guess I kind of overreacted, hmm?" she suggested after a moment or two.

"Yes, you did," Micah bluntly agreed.

A frown—mischievous though, not an unhappy one—settled over Blythe's features. "Would you think me terribly forward, Mr. Caine, if I were to ask you one or two questions?"

"How can I say without first hearing the questions, Ms. Donaldson?"

"In the months we've been apart, have you been stricken with some mysterious disease?"

"None that I know of."

"Were you injured in some way that would prevent you from enjoying sex?"

"No."

"Have you taken a vow of celibacy?"

Micah pressed his hips against Blythe's. "Does that feel like the sexual urge of a celibate?"

"I haven't the faintest notion." She grinned impishly.

"Believe me, it isn't."

"Care to offer me something more substantial than just your word?" she challenged brazenly.

"Oh yes." Micah groaned as he felt the silky softness of her slender foot easing in slow, provocative movements up and down his leg. He eased himself into place over Blythe, the hardness of his manhood finding its waiting counterpart, and entered her.

Blythe jerked her head to one side as an uncontrollable stab of exquisite pleasure permeated her. When Micah began a slow, rhythmic movement, she felt her breathing quicken and the blood in her veins intensify with each beat of her heart. Now the reason for her absolute devastation when she and Micah had parted became clearer. There had been the companionable aspect, of course, she reasoned as she rose dazedly from one glorious height in Micah's arms to another. But Micah had been her first lover, and even with her limited experience Blythe was sensible enough to know she'd picked a master in the art of lovemaking.

A multicolored shower of exploding brilliance flooded Blythe's mind and thoughts as she rode in the security of Micah's arms through that special valley to the ultimate completion only he could bring her.

The descent from that special world came about slowly and peacefully. They were two people exhausted but sated. Their skins gleamed with a silvery sheen of perspiration. Micah's head was cradled against the side of Blythe's neck, and one large, tan hand rested possessively over a pink, impudently tipped breast.

How long they lay dozing, Blythe wasn't sure. She awoke but kept her eyes closed when the steady breeze from the open window chilled her entire body. She then became aware that the weight that had been resting on her when she went to sleep was gone. Where was Micah? she wondered sleepily. Why had he slipped away?

The sudden warmth of a fleecy blanket falling into place across her body brought Blythe fully awake. She opened her dark eyes and stared at the tan giant standing beside the bed. He wore nothing but a towel that was knotted precariously around his hips and such a silly grin on his face that Blythe chuckled.

"You look like an idiot," she teased. She turned over onto her stomach and stretched.

Micah dropped down and sat cross-legged on the bed beside her. "But I feel like a king." He slid his hands beneath the blanket and ran them up and down the length of her back, finally coming to a stop on her buttocks. "Feeling rested?" he asked with a smirk.

Blythe opened one eye and regarded him suspiciously. "Spending the morning with you, Mr. Caine, can prove exhausting."

"True." Micah nodded solemnly, his eyes brimming with mischief. "But I can't believe you've grown so fainthearted in the months we've been apart."

With a rush of energy, Blythe sprang into a sitting position, dragging the sheet up to her chest with one hand while with the other she brushed back her hair that had fallen over her eyes. "Fishing for compliments, Micah?" she chortled.

"Of course I am." He grimaced comically. "I'm somewhat older than you are, you disrespectful wench. That being the case, I need to reassure myself that I'm still the greatest lover you've ever had."

"You make it sound like I installed a bill changer right outside my bedroom door," Blythe retorted. And then a peculiar gleam shone in her eyes. It couldn't be, she told herself. It couldn't be—could it? With a certain dignity and a flash of courage that she wouldn't have dared display almost two years ago—even if she'd had either—she leaned back on one elbow and thoughtfully regarded Micah. "I think what you're really trying to find out, in a ridiculously roundabout way, is whether or not Talbot was a good lover. Correct?"

"I can remember a time when you wouldn't have dreamed of asking me something like that," he said after a thoughtful pause. "But I suppose that's exactly what I was doing. I'd like to deny it, even try to cover it up, but I won't. I used to lie awake nights telling myself I didn't love you, dredging up every sort of unpleasant thoughts about you I could think of to try to keep from thinking about you being in Talbot's arms. If I'd known anything about witchcraft, I suppose I'd have cast a spell on you so that you'd have been miserable with him."

"Your spell would have been wasted," Blythe said quietly, feeling somewhat humbled herself at Micah's confession. "Realizing I'd made a mistake in marrying Talbot came very quickly. I'm not very proud of myself where he's concerned. I turned to him for all the wrong reasons. It was a very foolish and selfish move on my part."

Micah reached out and touched her cheek with the tips of his fingers. "I don't like to hear you put yourself down. You were hurt. You thought you'd been wronged, and you were looking for some way to regain your self-esteem."

"I realize all that now." Blythe grinned ruefully. "Unfortunately, Talbot realized it a few weeks after the wedding. All in all, he was pretty decent about the whole thing."

"Well, he did have rather a nice harem going to console him during his grieving, honey," Micah said bluntly.

"True," Blythe acknowledged with a shrug. "So between my reasons for marrying him and his extramarital affairs, I suppose that's why we're still friends of a sort. We don't see each other socially or anything like that, but there's no enmity between us. It's as though we both sort of used each other and got off

196

without a guilt trip hanging over us. Does that make any sense?"

"Yes. But I think I've heard enough about Talbot," Micah said decisively. "I know of a far more enjoyable thing I want to do right now than talk about your ex-husband." He caught the edge of the sheet and drew it down to her feet. "We have at least an hour and a half before I'm supposed to pick up the picnic basket. Can you possibly imagine what I have on my mind at the moment?"

Blythe laughed. "A blind man would know what you have on your mind," she said huskily as his arm slipped behind her and brought her close against his warm chest. The pebbled tips of her breasts became lost in the coarse hair on his chest, creating tiny, exquisite tremors of excitement that grew to a wild crescendo within her.

Micah's other hand became entangled in the short, dark curls covering her head, bringing it against his throat. "Is there any way I can possibly hope what's happening this morning means we're about to pick up where we left off when you decided I was being unfaithful?" he asked in a serious voice.

"Don't try to play dirty, Micah," Blythe still had enough presence of mind to warn him even though she could feel the web of passion encircling her securely within its tangling force. "We're two entirely different people now."

"Outwardly maybe, but emotionally we can still set fire to each other simply by letting our gazes lock. That will never change," he predicted forcefully.

"I suppose that's possible," Blythe whispered. She ran the tip of her tongue along the prominent protrusion of his collarbone, smiling to herself as she felt the quick jerk of his body. "There are other things besides sex that are needed in any relationship, don't you agree?" she murmured seductively.

Micah rolled over onto his back, his hands at Blythe's waist taking her with him and holding her in place on top of him while her legs neatly framed his longer, stronger ones. His features were taut with control. His eyes were narrowed against the aching need eating away at him. "I think we've talked too damn much," he rasped. "Though there is one last thing I think you should know."

"What's that?"

"I play dirty. I'll connive and go to any lengths necessary to get you back."

"I'll remember that."

"See that you do. In the meantime," he murmured as he caught her head and pulled it down so he could kiss her, "let's see what some plain, honest enticement can do for a really stubborn gal."

The tiny cove lay like a small green jewel along the stretch of white sandy beach. From the way the palm trees on either side sheltered it, Blythe dreamily assumed that it must have been laid out in the beginning by human hands. Perhaps in years past it had been used as a hideout for pirates.

A smile played around the edges of her lips as she tried to imagine Micah in the role of pirate. She found it was an easy picture to conjure up. With his talent for ordering people and his habit of getting his own way, he would have been perfectly at home, swinging through the air from deck to deck with a cutlass in one hand, swooping down on some helpless sailor.

"If I'm responsible for that smile, then you may continue wearing it. If it's about some other man, then erase it this instant." Micah dropped down beside her, making her squeal indignantly as drops of water were deliberately dribbled along her bikini-clad back.

"Go away." Blythe raised up on her elbows and glared at the man who was now occupying the plaid blanket with her. "You remind me of a large dog shaking the rain from his fur."

"Poor baby," Micah crooned as he leaned forward and dropped a kiss on her bare shoulder. One hand was hidden from Blythe, and a large piece of ice that he'd taken from the small ice chest was cupped in his palm. As his lips worked their special magic, he brought his hand to the hollow of her back, rubbing her honey-colored skin with the inside of his wrist. Lower and lower his wrist crept, until it was rubbing the edge of the bikini briefs. With slow, deliberate movements, he thrust the ice beneath the yellow triangle of material and quickly rolled to the far side of the blanket.

Blythe let forth a yell that would have done justice to a tribe of Indians. At the same instant she reached for her large plastic glass of lemonade over ice and flung the mixture at him.

Micah's "Damnation! That's pure ice!" and the hurried brushing of ice and drink from his head and the hair on his chest brought a malicious gleam of satisfaction to Blythe's eyes.

"Must you act so boorish?" she demanded with feigned haughtiness. "This is the first chance I've had to work on my tan since I've been in Florida, and you have to spoil it by resorting to boyish shenanigans."

"You didn't do too bad yourself," Micah said with a grin. He was rubbing his head with a thick towel and leering lasciviously at the brevity of Blythe's bikini bra. "I especially liked it when you swerved around so quickly. It gave me a most attractive view of your lovely breasts."

Blythe blushed to the roots of her hair as she sat beneath the amused indulgence of Micah's gaze. He was right, she was forced to admit, they only had to look at each other and a special fire would spring to life in their eyes. "I hate to ruin an otherwise perfect day, but I have a meeting at five-thirty," he told her. "I'll take a walk down the beach and allow you forty-five minutes to your sunbathing. Okay?"

"Forty-five minutes will be fine," Blythe murmured and dropped her gaze from his open, more challenging one. One minute she felt confident and assured; the next, she was as unsure of herself as a baby.

The morning, and the idyllic manner in

which it had been spent, was proof enough
that sexually they were still very much at-
tuned to each other. Blythe had no quarrel
with that. But how long could a relationship
survive if the attraction was purely sexual?

CHAPTER THIRTEEN

She knew it was silly, but during the drive
back to the hotel, visions of the lovely Kristi
Barr in a heavy embrace with Micah kept flit-
ting through Blythe's mind. Blythe had to bite
her tongue to keep from asking him who he
was meeting at five-thirty.

Don't be so foolish, she lectured herself
sternly. He is the head of a multifaceted corporation, and he sees any number of people
during the course of a day, pretty women as
well as men.

But no amount of reasoning could assuage
the sinking feeling, the heavy hand of jealousy that caught her heart and refused to let
go. Kristi was beautiful. She lived in a world as

fast paced as Micah's was. Blythe had read various accounts of the singer's affairs with different men. It didn't help her peace of mind to know that for the next six weeks, Micah would be in daily contact with Kristi Barr. Knowing her own vacation was not nearly that long didn't make Blythe feel one bit better.

But she wasn't even sure of her feelings for him, her critical conscience scoffed as the silent dialogue became more heated and intense. She had gone to bed with him very willingly, she had to admit. And every time he was around her, she all but fell apart, trembling like a young girl when he touched her. *Stop it*, she told herself, it was about time she stopped vascillating and accepted reality, accepted what she felt for Micah.

"Is it really that bad, honey?" Micah broke the silence hovering between them. He reached out and grasped her hand to lightly squeeze it.

"I'm sorry," Blythe spluttered, her cheeks turning an attractive shade of pink. It was as if Micah could see into her very mind. "What did you say?"

"Nothing of importance." He chuckled. "If

I can get loose in time, will you have dinner with me later?"

"Why shouldn't you be able to get free?" she asked, making the question sound like a challenge.

Micah shot her a quizzical look, then turned his attention back to the road. "There are a number of people I have to see," he spoke calmly, far more calmly than he was feeling. He'd seen jealousy before, Micah thought with a surge of excitement, and he was positive that it was that same emotion that put a peculiar stoniness in Blythe's gaze and a rigid set to her lips. She looked ready to commit murder—his!

"Does one of them happen to be Kristi Barr?"

"As a matter of fact, I am seeing Kristi, along with her manager. She's made a number of changes in her show that have been quite expensive. They want me to absorb a certain percentage of the cost since our contract says I'll provide adequate lighting and staging, and they claim the changes were made for the specific setting offered by the Crystal Room. Unfortunately, they've revamped their entire show, right down to costumes, and they're pretending to be surprised that I'm not overjoyed at the additional amount of money involved."

"In other words, they're trying to rip you off?" Blythe suggested with a trace of ice in her voice. It would serve him right, she was thinking. If he was so besotted as to let Kristi Barr bat those ridiculously long lashes at him and fall for her story, then he should have to pay through the nose!

"In a manner of speaking." Micah grinned. "Oh, it's all friendly and above board, but it does take a bit of negotiating."

"In other words, the entire matter is nothing more than a big farce," Blythe scoffed. Friendly and above board indeed! It was downright pathetic, she thought maliciously, that a grown, supposedly intelligent man could allow a pretty face to fleece him like a shorn lamb. "If they know you aren't going to give more money than the contract states, why bother?"

"It's not quite like that. It's called business, honey." Micah smiled. "Kristi is a good friend," he said tongue-in-cheek. "I signed her back when she wasn't a star, and I treated her fairly. Her manager, besides being something of a character, is one of the best in the business. This meeting will be a chance for us

206

both to bend a little. I'll make one or two concessions, they'll do the same, and we'll both come away feeling like we got the best end of the deal. In other areas of the country it's called horse-trading. Nobody will be hurt nor feel they've been taken advantage of."

Blythe shrugged. "Sounds like a lot of wasted time to me. Will Miss Barr and her manager be the only people you see this evening?" Lord, she thought disgustedly, she was beginning to sound like a broken record.

"I'm afraid not. There are a couple of people flying in from the Bahamas. They represent a consortium interested in buying me out —which is amusing, since I haven't the slightest desire to sell. Their offer could eventually turn into a fight if they try to force a takeover. But for now I think a couple of drinks tonight and a longer meeting tomorrow will be all that's necessary."

"Why don't we just forget about dinner? If either of your appointments run late, it will be well into the evening before you're free. I think I'd rather have an early dinner anyway."

Micah started to argue but thought better of it. He knew that Blythe was ready to explode with self-righteous indignation. He almost laughed out loud as he imagined the thoughts milling around in her head. In all fairness, he reasoned, he could have rescheduled the appointments, but now he was glad he hadn't. It wasn't often that he found himself in such a position, and he decided it was about time he became involved in a little horse-trading with the flinty-eyed, scowling beauty sitting beside him.

Blythe was seething, but short of lashing out at Micah—and making a total fool of herself in the process—there was little she could do. She'd fallen into a trap of her own design. Micah hadn't the slightest idea why she'd gone to bed with him . . . For that matter, she sighed rather forlornly, neither had she. But she was positive of one thing: she could no longer hide behind the shield that she didn't care for Micah. She did care, deeply. Being with him made a cloudy day appear as if the sun were at its zenith. His presence could brighten the dullest moment, even when she was engaged in a battle of wills with him. In short, she loved him. Only this time, she was wise enough to know that there was more than just sex in a relationship.

For almost two years she'd denied herself the pleasure of his company. She would probably still be doing so now if he hadn't taken matters into his own hands. As usual, when Micah decided to act, it had far-reaching effects. Well, he'd certainly acted. Only days ago she'd been relatively happy with her life in Mobile; her shop and her family had been the mainstays in her life. And then Micah had reappeared. It hadn't been the first time she'd seen him, but always before he'd gone away after dropping in on her or visiting longer with her aunts. Not so this time, she quietly reflected. This time he'd truly turned her life into a circus sideshow. There were decisions to be made, decisions she wasn't even ready to acknowledge were necessary.

When the dark green Ferrari hummed to a stop in the circular entrance to the hotel, Blythe opened the door and had stepped out before Micah even had time to reach forward and switch off the ignition key.

"I hope your meetings go well," she said casually while she pulled out her straw purse and canvas carryall from the car. "Perhaps you'll be able to give me thirty minutes of your time tomorrow. I can't pretend to be interested in taking over your corporation, nor am I interested in performing in that stuffed shirt Renaldo's Crystal Room. But if you find yourself in need of some conversation, a drink maybe, then give me a call."

"Thank you." Micah nodded courteously, struggling not to laugh. "I'll make it a point to ask my secretary if I can possibly squeeze you in." He gave her a gleeful look, then started the Ferrari and roared down the drive and into the private parking area reserved for him and Stephen.

As Blythe showered and dressed, she was reliving the events that had taken place during the rather remarkable day.

But a look of chagrin washed over her face as she turned off her hair dryer and straightened. She didn't really want to see her reflection in the mirror above the dressing table. It was a wonder there wasn't a sign on her forehead telling the world that she'd made a bloody fool of herself for most of the day. Not only had she spent the greater part of the morning in Micah's arms, even the picnic had been delayed while they made love again.

Micah had seemed insatiable. It was as if his need for her were something he'd barely been able to hold in check. His physical hunger for her had flung Blythe into a whirlwind that was only just beginning to dissipate.

She dropped the dryer onto the counter

with a thud and began combing her soft curls into some sort of order, sighing with disgust as she did so. Not with what had taken place between her and Micah—never that, she told herself. Making love with him had been every bit as wonderful as she had remembered. No, she told herself, the disgust was with the confusion, the mess she'd made of her life as well as Micah's. Why hadn't Amanda or Carrie made her sit down and listen to reason when she'd broken her engagement so quickly? she wondered. But would she have listened then? Would she have done a single thing differently?

Blythe stood still, her thoughts going back to the event that had turned her life upside down. She'd been shocked when she walked into Micah's suite that early evening so many months ago. The sight of the blonde running her red-tipped fingers over his chest, then down his back to his hips, had been like a knife that was being plunged into Blythe's heart.

She'd cried out silently for Micah to fight, to push the woman away from him, but he hadn't. He had stood passively, neither taking part nor repulsing the blonde. It was Blythe's strangled sound of surprise that brought a reaction from him. All he'd seen was her pale, startled face as she whirled around and ran from the room.

Remembering wasn't going to solve her problems nor help her make the right decisions, she finally told herself. Remembering only brought pain. There was also one other very important aspect to consider, she conceded. She really hadn't the foggiest idea what she wanted with Micah. It had only been a short time since she'd admitted she still cared for him. Only a half-hour since she'd admitted she still loved him. It was all happening so quickly, how could she possibly make a snap decision about what she wanted to do with the rest of her life?

"God!" Blythe gave a quick shake of her head. "I am quickly and thoroughly going stark raving mad. Now, to add insult to injury, I'm holding conversations with myself. I need to be around other people, to hear voices. Even snooty Renaldo would be a welcome change."

Blythe finished dressing and went to the Crystal Room for dinner. Frankly, she told herself as she entered the lovely, gleaming atmosphere, she wasn't that hungry. But for the life of her, she wasn't going to sit in her room like a pouting child. What was really galling her, she admitted, was that Micah and she had enjoyed such a beautiful day, and he had ruined it by casually informing her he had an evening full of appointments. He *was* the head of the damn organization, wasn't he? she fumed. The string of hotels belonged to him, so why couldn't he delegate some of his precious authority to an assistant? At least for one lousy evening!

With a purposeful gleam in her eye, Blythe looked around pointedly. She spotted Renaldo and then watched him mask the grimace that almost surfaced when he saw her. The first thought that ran through her mind was that he reminded her of a cornered rat. For some unfathomable reason, she and Renaldo had immediately disliked each other, and she decided that no amount of pretending on either one's part was likely to change the situation. As she waited for him to mince his way across the room and stand before her, Blythe couldn't help but wonder if a spot for Renaldo could be found in Kristi Barr's entourage at the end of her engagement.

"Ms. Donaldson," he said politely—certainly not pleasantly, Blythe grinned to herself. "Mr. Caine didn't tell me that you would be dining with us this evening."

Mr. Caine doesn't tell you everything, she was tempted to snarl. Instead, she smiled. "Really? How remiss of him," she said coolly. "I suppose I'll have his usual table." Rather than wait for the proffered elbow, Blythe swept forward like a duchess, the long, silky skirt of her dress lightly billowing out behind her in a delicate cloud of pale rose. Her shoulders, one bare, the other partially covered by a one-shouldered strap, glowed in the brilliant crystal light that shone like millions of tiny stars in the room. At her throat she wore her mother's pearls. On her wrist was the gold bracelet Micah had given her.

The number of male glances that lingered on her as she passed their tables were many. One man looked especially intrigued.

The pained Renaldo held Blythe's chair, his back rigid. The moment she was seated, he did a perfect goose-step to the left. Blythe held her breath, fully expecting him to click his heels together.

"May I get you something to drink?" he asked, the epitome of the perfect host.

"A glass of white wine."

"Is there a vintage you prefer?"

"No," Blythe told him without the slightest apology in her voice. "I don't know a good wine from a bad one. I'll leave the choice up to you."

"Of course," Renaldo murmured.

"Blythe? Am I seeing straight? Have you finally forgiven old Micah for trying to sleep with all the women in the county?"

Blythe almost fell off her chair, she whirled around so quickly. "Stephen!" she cried, just as she was caught up in a bear hug by a slightly smaller version of Micah. "Micah said you were coming," she managed when she could get her face free of a chest as wide as Micah's.

"Well, to tell you the truth, I wasn't sure when I was going to get here. I met the prettiest little gal—"

"Hush," Blythe laughed, holding up a hand as if to ward off an evil spell. "I don't want to know a single thing about any of your women." Stephen released her with a deep chuckle, then looked at the wholly disapproving Renaldo, who had been observing the scene with obvious distaste.

"Still trying to intimidate people, eh, 'Naldo?" Stephen quipped. He clapped the much shorter man on the shoulder and then sat down. "I can use a Scotch on the rocks."

"Of course, sir," Renaldo replied stiffly, then fled as if the hounds of hell were nipping at his heels.

"Damn strange fellow." Stephen frowned as he watched the headwaiter disappear, then shrugged philosophically. He turned back to Blythe, his face wreathed with a smile. "Seeing you here is one hell of a surprise, kid, and a mighty pleasant one at that. How did Micah manage it? The last thing I knew about you two, you wouldn't even give him the time of day."

"That's what I like about you, Stephen," Blythe replied with a smile. "You are the soul of tact. You exemplify the true essence of the word. You enter a room, and tranquillity surrounds you. People are lulled to sleep by your very presence."

CHAPTER FOURTEEN

"And all this time I thought you were a friend of mine." Stephen smiled again, not in the least bothered by Blythe's teasing. "Seriously though, what are you doing here? This is one of Micah's hotels, you know."

Blythe tipped her head forward and grinned. "I'll have you know I'm here because my two aunts were the 'winners' in a contest sponsored by this very establishment."

"Contest?"

"Of course. Weren't you aware of the magnanimous gesture made by your brother?" she asked innocently.

"My brother never does anything without a

217

very good reason. I think the contest story is a crock of bull."

Blythe nodded. "It was. What Micah really did was concoct this fictitious contest. The only hitch was, my aunts were the only entrants—unbeknownst to them, of course. They were instant winners of a two-week vacation at The Palms. Since they'd recently been witnesses of a rather nasty hit-and-run accident, they weren't at their best emotionally, and they insisted they couldn't possibly make the trip without me. I've even found myself wondering if Micah had anything to do with that poor man being run down."

"What man?" Stephen frowned.

"Oh," Blythe shook her head dismissively, "I shouldn't have brought up that subject. My aunts were on one of their contest jaunts several days ago. While waiting their turn to be shown through some condominiums, they struck up a conversation with a gentleman who was also waiting. After talking for fifteen or twenty minutes, he suddenly jumped to his feet and began to run toward the parking lot. A car came zooming out of nowhere and ran over him. The driver made no attempt to stop. From a newspaper account I read in this morning's paper, it seems the man was an accountant. He was also due to testify for the government later this month. Seems the corporation for which he worked had been systematically bilking the government of millions for several years."

"Sounds like your accountant friend had friends who didn't want him to testify, doesn't it?" Stephen grimaced.

"Not my friend, please. I never even met the poor man."

"Well, at least it's nice to know you were kidding about Micah having had him done in."

"I can see you still believe in getting right to the heart of a matter. For your information, I didn't really believe any such thing."

"Ah, protecting Micah from his thick-skinned brother, eh?"

"Nothing so gallant, I assure you." Blythe chuckled. "Neither of you is in need of protection from anyone."

At that moment Renaldo placed their drinks in front of them and vanished before either of them had a chance to say a word to him.

"For the life of me, I can't figure out why Micah keeps that sourpuss." Stephen slowly shook his head. He looked back to Blythe, his gaze running appreciatively over each part of her that was visible above the table. "You're looking as lovely as you did the last time I saw you. I thought grief and unrequited love were supposed to make a woman look old."

"Thank you, but what in the world are you talking about?"

"These past months of longing for my brother."

"I see—I think." Blythe frowned. "Er, where did you get the idea I was pining away for Micah?"

"Why, from the big guy himself," Stephen replied mockingly. "Every time he got soused. Being his only relative, it seemed to be my lot in life to console him. I tell you, there've been times when I've seriously considered kidnapping you and stashing you and big brother together in some remote cabin and throwing away the key."

"How interesting," Blythe murmured dryly. "But instead of locking me away with him, why not throw in a couple of your women? You might even include Kristi Barr, since he seems to be so fond of her."

"Uh-oh," Stephen mused with thoughtful anticipation. "Methinks the green-eyed monster has dared rear its ugly head among us. Is there something I should know? Let me put it another way. Are you here purely as a guest with your aunts, or is there something going on between you and Micah?"

"I don't believe you." Blythe stared disbelievingly at him. "Isn't anything sacred to you?"

"Not much." He shrugged, not at all insulted. "I simply look at a problem, decide the simplest way to a solution, then damn the torpedoes and full speed ahead."

"Well, as much as I hate to disappoint you," Blythe replied guardedly, "I'm neither a problem nor a submarine."

"Okay," he said good-naturedly, "so I'm a bit brash. But I do know that Micah is still very much in love with you. And I wasn't kidding about pouring him into bed on occasion. Pity was something I'd never associated with my big brother until I saw him almost come apart after you broke your engagement."

"It wasn't easy for me, either," Blythe said in self-defense.

"You must have healed pretty fast, honey. You were married within four months, weren't you?"

"Yes," she said decisively, "and for all the wrong reasons."

"I tried to see you to tell you that what had happened really wasn't Micah's fault. The blonde was my friend." He looked a bit sheepish. "I'll be the first to admit she wasn't discriminating in the least, but she was honest, and she filled a void for me at that particular time in my life. My only regret is that her 'friendliness' was the reason for your break with Micah."

"Don't worry, Stephen," Blythe said softly. "I think Micah and I have gotten beyond that hurdle. I'll admit there was quite a while there when I believed the very worst. But time and Micah's persistence began to make me wonder. Once that happened, I asked myself some questions. I didn't particularly like the answers, but I accepted them."

"And now?" Stephen persisted. "Since Micah finagled a way of getting you here, have the two of you resolved your differences? Are you going to be my sister-in-law?"

"Dear Lord," Blythe replied in feigned horror. "I hadn't thought of that. I'm going to my room and begin packing this instant."

"Listen, toots, every woman should be so lucky. I'll make a great addition to any family.

Just imagine, I can chauffeur your aunts to all sorts of interesting places."

"In their station wagon?" Blythe asked innocently.

"Oh, hell. Why can't you talk them into getting something with a little more class?"

"The station wagon has class to them," Blythe chuckled. "Besides, don't you think we're jumping the gun slightly? Micah and I still have some problems to work out."

"You will," Stephen promised, "believe me. By the way, where is the boss? I tried calling his place but there was no answer. It's not like him to leave you to dine on your own."

"I haven't spent a bundle on costume or lighting changes that I hope to recoup by playing on Micah's sympathy."

"I beg your pardon?" A totally blank look came over Stephen's face.

"Kristi Barr. She's beginning an engagement here in the Crystal Room tomorrow."

"Yes, I know. She's very popular, always brings in an excellent house. But what's that got to do with you eating alone?"

"Kristi and her manager are meeting with Micah this evening. After he's through with them, he's seeing two gentlemen representing some consortium that wants to buy him out. If he can possibly work it in, he might be able to drop by and have dessert with me."

"I see."

"Good. Now that we've settled that little problem, would you care to have dinner with me?"

"I'd be honored. There's just one thing, though."

"What?"

"Why don't we go somewhere else? I see enough of this place during the day. I know the perfect little club about an hour's drive from here that has an excellent band and dancing. The food isn't bad, either. Game?"

"And how," Blythe quickly replied, her enthusiasm coming more from loneliness and frustration than from any genuine desire to go dancing. Actually, she thought fleetingly as she reached for her purse and rose to her feet, she was tired. But something deep within her prevented her from eating a quiet dinner and then obediently waiting in her room for Micah. If she couldn't be first in his life, then she didn't want to be there at all.

The club Stephen chose was crowded but nice. The band, a regular on a late-night television show, played a wide range of hits, from the forties to the present popular numbers. Stephen went about his dancing much the same as he did everything else Blythe had seen him do, with enormous gusto. She did nothing to stop the smile that came to her lips when her imagination took on the unbelievable task of picturing Stephen falling in love.

"It isn't nice to keep a silly grin plastered on your face the entire time you're dancing with me," he complained. "I might get a complex."

"Bull," Blythe scoffed. "If I were to tell you what I was thinking about, you'd laugh as well."

"Try me."

"As improbable as it may seem, I was trying to picture you in love. I was wondering if you'd go about it as enthusiastically as everything else you do."

"Damn, Blythe." He paled. "Don't even talk that way. The thought of some woman managing my life like a drill sergeant sends me into a cold sweat."

"But I thought you liked women." Now that she'd found out what a fraud he really was, Blythe was ready to get down to some serious teasing.

"I do, kid, I do. But only as long as I can love 'em and leave 'em."

"Hmm," she frowned. "You and your brother have more than just looks in common."

"Ah, come on, honey." Stephen tried to reason with her. "I'll admit Micah has always liked women, but when you and he were together, he never even looked at another female."

"Oh, you can stop trying to convince me that Micah was faithful, Stephen. I've long since realized that I was the dope of the year for the way I handled the cute little scene with your blonde friend and Micah. However"—she looked grim—"there are still women in his life to be dealt with, aren't there? Like Miss Barr, for instance, and her after-five appointments? Just who the hell does she think she is?"

"But that's business."

"In a pig's eye!"

"She always makes appointments in the evening," Stephen said with a rush, then wished he could cut out his tongue as Blythe's expression became grimmer. *Damn Micah*, he was thinking. Why the hell didn't he tell Kristi Barr to go fly a kite? Blythe was on the verge of exploding, and Stephen wasn't sure he knew what to do with her.

"Then Mr. Caine is going to have to learn how to rearrange his schedule, isn't he?" she ground out, daring Stephen to disagree with her.

He nodded his head. "Excellent idea. Don't know why he hasn't thought of it. I'll put it to him first thing in the morning. How about another Passion's Embrace?" God! If he did anything to make Blythe run away again, Micah would kill him.

"Sounds good. Make it a double."

"Blythe, nobody asks for a double Passion's Embrace. It's Nick's own recipe, and a powerful one at that."

"Really, Stephen," she regally told him, "I do think I'm capable of handling a little rum."

"If you say so, kid." He caught Nick's eye, pointed to their glasses, then held up two fingers over Blythe's. The bartender raised his dark brows, then shrugged.

When the cocktail waitress arrived with the drinks, Stephen sat Blythe's before her with misgivings. He'd had more than his usual quota of alcohol for the evening, and Blythe was well on her way to getting bombed. That left only one course open to him. He could either get a taxi to take them back to the hotel, or he could have someone from The Palms come and get them. Pete, the kid who parked the guests' cars at the hotel, would be perfect he decided. He excused himself and went to the pay phone, asking Pete to pick them up in an hour or so.

After his conversation, Stephen returned to the table. He and Blythe resumed their dancing, conversation, and good time with renewed enthusiasm.

No wonder Micah had fallen for Blythe, Stephen decided some time later as he guided her through a pattern of intricate footwork during a rather jazzy number. She was pretty, intelligent, and fun to be with. He twirled her around, then made a rather unsteady grab at her so she wouldn't lose her sense of direction. But instead of Blythe staying where she was and then gliding back to him the way she was supposed to, she suddenly flew across the floor in the wake of a tall man, the crowd of dancers parting before him like the Red Sea.

"Oh, hell!" a bleary-eyed Stephen muttered as he recognized his brother's back rather than Pete's. With characteristic indifference, he made his way to the table where Micah was standing beside a visibly angry

Blythe. "Glad you could finally join us, Micah." He tapped his brother on the shoulder, then took a seat and calmly observed the star-crossed pair. "Something wrong?"

"In the future when you plan one of your little outings, I'd appreciate it if one of you would be considerate enough to leave word where you're going." Micah spoke in a voice like the flicking of a rawhide whip. He turned the full glint of his blistering gaze on Blythe. "Considering several incidents that have occurred within the last few days, I had no way of knowing what happened to you until Pete heard from Stephen."

"Sorry." Blythe smiled icily. Her double Passion's Embrace had left her tongue feeling as if it were two inches thick. "We just naturally thought you would be tied up with Kinky Bart."

"Who?" Micah frowned.

"You heard her," Stephen told his brother with a perfectly straight face. "That Kinky Bart woman that sings. Really, Micah. You should start scheduling your appointments in the morning, you know. You really should." Stephen nodded as if he were trying to convince himself of something very important but was unable to remember exactly what it was.

"I don't believe this." Micah slowly shook his dark blond head, looking from one to the other. "You're both as potted as the proverbial palm."

"Loaded to the gills," Blythe concurred.

"I second that motion," a still-nodding Stephen chimed in.

By gritting his teeth and exerting more patience than he had ever dreamed himself capable of, Micah got them back to The Palms, though not before he'd been entertained by the duo with several little ditties that struck both of them as being extremely funny. But they weren't funny in the least to Micah—at least, not at the moment. It made him mad as hell that, by merely smiling, Stephen could take Blythe out to dinner and dancing. The only thing he was pleased about was that his brother had had the good sense not to drive.

When they got back to the hotel, after sending Stephen on his way to his bungalow, Micah guided an unsteady Blythe to her room. Once inside, he locked the door and then began to undress her.

"I'm perfectly capable of doing that for myself," she told him haughtily, trying for the fourth time to open the simple clasp of the bracelet on her wrist while he took care of the buttons and hooks.

"Oh, sure," he agreed, giving in to the urge to grin. She was as drunk as she'd probably ever been, but Blythe Donaldson wasn't about to allow herself to become a common, ordinary drunk. Drunk as a lord, she had style, he thought, and he liked that.

"Would you mind lifting your right foot?" he asked politely.

"Why?"

"Because you're standing on your dress, and I'd like to hang it up."

"Nonsense." She grasped his arm with both hands and then barely lifted her foot an inch off the floor, indifferent to the fact that she was attired in a scanty pair of beige panties and a tiny strapless bra. "See?"

"My mistake," Micah said solemnly. "Why don't you sit on the bed? Then we can take off your shoes without fear of you falling."

Blythe frowned as she considered the question. It sounded reasonable enough to her, she supposed, but she didn't like his tone of voice. She opened her mouth to tell him so, then promptly forgot what she was angry about. She shrugged, then took three wobbly steps and dropped down onto the edge of the bed, her head spinning like a top. Trying to focus her eyes was a major undertaking. "You should watch that Renaldo character."

"Why's that?"

"Because I remember ordering one glass of wine from him, and loo—look at me now."

"Shameful," Micah sympathized. He removed not only her shoes but her bra as well. "I'll speak to him tomorrow. In the meantime, hold up your arms and let me slip this gown on you. I'm sure you'll be more comfortable."

"Thank you, Micah," Blythe said primly, nude except for the sheer panties. "I really do love you, you know. I'm afraid, though, that you'll have to do something about that Kinky woman."

"Believe me, I'll take care of it first thing tomorrow," Micah said huskily. There was an extremely satisfied expression on his face as he turned back the spread and settled Blythe into the bed. Then he removed his own clothes and got in beside her.

He gathered her close in his arms. His mind was busy trying to figure the next move in this game of the heart they were playing. Bit by bit, Blythe was turning back to him, and that pleased him. He'd been startled by the depth of his jealousy when he found out she'd gone off with Stephen. Though Stephen was his own brother, Micah wasn't able to control the cold fear of losing Blythe again.

CHAPTER FIFTEEN

The first coherent thought Blythe was able to
formulate when she awoke and opened her
eyes was that someone had mistaken her head
for a vacant lot and was now building an
apartment complex on it.

"Oh, my God," she moaned. Both hands
went up to cradle her head. She tried closing
her eyes tightly, but even that simple flexing
of muscles brought excruciating pain.

The pounding grew louder, and she was
convinced she was going to die at any moment. Her stomach reminded her of a time,
long ago, when her parents had taken her to a
fair. She'd ridden all sorts of wild rides and
was royally sick on the way home. She was just

that sick now, she told herself. God! If only that awful pounding would go away. It sounded as if it were right in the room with her.

Suddenly, the pounding stopped. Blythe gave a muffled groan, then covered her head with a pillow. But her reprieve was short-lived, for now she was positive she could hear a scratching noise. It sounded as if ten cats were using her door for a scratching post.

When a hand dropped onto her foot, Blythe almost screamed. She'd had one or two hangovers before and was fairly well acquainted with the various noises one was capable of hearing during them. But none of her after-the-party moments had ever had a hand in them, accompanied by a hard shake—which was happening at that precise moment. A booming voice followed.

"Move your cute little behind over, toots."

Stephen. No one else in the world had such a way with words. Blythe was almost convinced that a tiny smile wouldn't completely kill her. She tried it, then moaned.

"Come on," he chuckled. He removed the pillow, the blue spread, the blanket, and finally the sheet from her face. "Christ! Are you trying to smother yourself?"

"Must you shout?" Blythe glared at him as best she could with her only eye that would open. "What on earth did you slip into my drink last night?"

"Me?" Stephen hooted. "That's a laugh. You were guzzling Nick's Passion's Embraces like it was your last night on earth."

"I think it quite likely was," she said faintly. "I honestly think I'm dying."

"Well, open your eyes, honey. I've got the perfect concoction for a hangover right here in this little glass."

"Is that what you took to make you sound so nauseatingly cheerful?" Blythe asked hopefully.

" 'Fraid not. I'm never bothered with hangovers," Stephen confessed with his usual candor. "Something to do with a chemical imbalance, I suppose." He shook his dark head in quiet sympathy as he watched Blythe push herself into a halfway-sitting position and then struggle to open both eyes.

"Oh!"

"That bad, huh?"

"Ten times worse," she moaned.

"Then drink this, and in thirty minutes you won't even know you had a drink last night."

"Oh, do you really—" Her voice failed her

as she caught sight of the tall glass of red liquid he was holding before her. "Did you have to double the recipe?"

"One serving, I promise. Come on"—Stephen grinned—"don't be a coward."

A sudden noise from the doorway caused them both to turn and look that way—Stephen turned easily, while Blythe made the move more cautiously and painfully.

"Getting an early start on your plans for the evening?" Micah quipped sourly as he dismissed the waiter and then pushed the food cart into the room and closed the door.

"Of course," Stephen came back without the slightest hesitation. "Right after we have a wild thirty-minute sexual fling, that is." He turned back to Blythe, summarily dismissing Micah and his rotten temper. "I'm not leaving until you drink every drop of this, toots."

Finding that no one was even the slightest bit intimidated by his appearance, Micah had no recourse but to sit on the opposite side of the bed and watch the proceedings. In spite of wanting to tear a strip off Stephen and Blythe for frightening the hell out of him last night with their disappearing act, he was still forced to admit he'd never seen a more unlikely team in his life. The trouble was, his eyes narrowed thoughtfully as he watched their antics, if they were to put their heads together, there was no telling what they could get into. That being the case, Micah decided he was definitely going to find the time to be available for Blythe. There was something about Stephen that women found attractive, and he sure as hell wasn't about to let Blythe fall into that trap.

"Is that concoction really necessary?" Micah asked. Even he would have had trouble downing such a dose. From Blythe's green color, he had a feeling she would never make it.

"Guaranteed to make one feel like a new person in thirty minutes." Stephen smiled. "Besides, your fragile little flower here drank enough rum last night to take the hair off everybody's tongue."

"What did she drink?"

"Double Passion's Embraces."

"And you let her?" Micah yelled.

"How the hell was I supposed to stop her? She's over twenty-one, you know. Now, if you'll excuse us, we'll get back to the problem at hand." He pointed a finger at the silent Blythe. "Either you drink willingly, or I'll hold your nose and pour it down your throat."

"You wouldn't dare," she said.

"Try me."

Micah watched the Mexican standoff and was really surprised when he saw Blythe raise the glass to her lips and swallow the drink. He looked at Stephen with new respect in his eyes. "Remind me to have a talk with you real soon."

"Anytime." Stephen grinned. Then he said to Blythe, "Give yourself a few minutes, and then go on about your business. By the time you've showered and are ready for breakfast, you'll be fine."

"You do know I'll get you back, don't you?" Blythe glared at him.

"Of course. However, I would think you'd want to be nice to me. When you finally marry my big brother, we'll be related—I might even live with the two of you from time to time." He smiled cockily at the two people staring daggers at him and then left the room.

"I only have two aunts, both of whom you seem to care for," Blythe said after several quiet seconds had passed. "Please tell me Stephen is adopted and that his natural mother is launching a massive search for him."

"It sounds like a wonderful idea"—Micah chuckled—"but I'm afraid I'm stuck with him." He reached out and caught her hand resting on the sheet and held it. "How are you really feeling this morning?"

"Awful, but I'm sure I'll make it. It would be too kind to let me die." She grinned. "Was I dreaming last night or did you sleep with me?" she asked on a more serious note. He looked so good to her, she thought. His hair was still damp from his shower, and he smelled fresh and clean. Her gaze ran over his pale yellow pullover shirt with a narrow blue stripe and navy pants. He was dressed casually, and she wondered if he had canceled his meeting today with the men from the Bahamas.

"You weren't dreaming," Micah finally answered. He hadn't spoken while she stared at him for fear of breaking her concentration. There was something different about her this morning, and he needed time to try and figure out what it was. Suddenly, he was amused. Every time he'd seen Blythe in the last two or three days, there'd been something different about her. He was beginning to wonder if she'd really changed that much, or if—as she'd pointed out during one of their talks—they were beginning to get to know each other better.

"Why did you stay?"

"Because I wanted to be near you. I was also afraid you might be sick or need something during the night."

Blythe smiled gently. "Other people have hangovers and manage alone."

"I'm proud of them," Micah said gruffly. "But in your case you didn't have to manage. I was here to do it for you."

"I'm supposed to be angry with you, did you know that?" she asked rather crisply.

Micah chuckled and nodded. "I think I have a pretty good idea why. Does it have anything to do with Kinky Bart?"

"Who?" Blythe stared at him.

"Last night, you were just full of cute remarks about Kinky Bart, English translation: Kristi Barr."

"Oh." Blythe silently mulled over this new and surprising revelation. "Well, at any rate, I'm not mad any longer. I realize you have a business to run, and I should be more understanding."

"That's nice," Micah replied silkily, "and I do appreciate your concern. But I've had my secretary rearrange my schedule for the next week and a half. Unless it's an emergency, I'll be able to spend every evening with you, and a few hours during each day."

"Really?"

"Yes."

"How nice." She swung her feet to the floor and stood. She couldn't put a name to it, but having him with her seemed very important at the moment. "Will you wait while I shower and have breakfast with me?"

Micah got up and walked around the bed to take her in his arms. His hands ran seductively over the satin softness of the gown as he molded the garment to the shape of her figure. "Wild horses couldn't drag me out of here." His mouth swooped down and claimed hers, leaving a trembling, breathless Blythe to make her way awkwardly to the shower.

The day passed in a flurry of laughter and activity for Blythe. She was constantly being teased or kept busy by Micah or Stephen or both. It was only toward late afternoon that the first hint of trouble surfaced.

"I know we've already made plans for dinner," Micah scowled, "but I have to keep one appointment. It involves a man's future." They were standing on the balcony of his suite watching the sunset.

"Don't worry," Blythe assured him, although she was disappointed. "I'll have an early dinner, watch some TV, and wait for you."

"The last time you said that, you wound up gorging yourself on Passion's Embraces and dancing all night with my brother."

"I felt used," Blythe replied without thinking, and then she was quite surprised to learn that that really had been how she'd felt.

"Because we'd made love?"

"Yes. Funny, but until this very moment, I wasn't aware of why I felt such an incredible urge to lash out at you," she confessed.

"And you do now?"

"Yes."

"Do you trust me, Blythe?" Micah asked, his narrowed gaze watching her face for the slightest change in expression.

"I'm learning to," she said honestly, "and I'm trying to. You're no longer the godlike man I used to think you were. I finally had to acknowledge that." She smiled a little sadly. "It was painful letting go of my fantasy, but I'm finding I like the mortal you a whole lot better."

CHAPTER SIXTEEN

Long after Micah had gone to his meeting and Blythe was on her own, she paused and looked back on all the times they'd spent together during the last few days. She was beginning to see him in a new light, and it wasn't an unattractive one at all.

With a spring in her step that bespoke her good mood, Blythe let herself out of Micah's private quarters and headed for a long walk on the beach.

She still couldn't believe how easily everything seemed to fall into place once she had stopped fighting him. And though the tranquility that surrounded their relationship at the moment certainly couldn't be expected to last indefinitely, Blythe was heartened by it. She knew that anything beyond it was strictly in the hands of the gods. So far, the things she'd learned about Micah, things she'd never bothered with before, had proved to be nice. Once she'd taken the time to put her fear and her overactive imagination on hold, she'd found that he was a very vulnerable, loving individual. One of his dreams was for a home and a family.

A soft smile played at the edges of Blythe's lips as she walked along the sand, her mind conjuring up all sorts of pictures of Micah playing ball with their son or their tiny daughter patiently waiting for him to tell her a story.

Wafflehead! Miss Wafflehead of the year! Give the poor man a chance, her conscience began shrieking at her. It was only the second day of a renewed affair, and she already had the man pegged with children and a vine-covered cottage God knew where, while she stood in the doorway nodding approval.

Blythe had to laugh at herself. She was rather jumping the gun. Or was she? Hadn't Micah said he wanted them to pick up where they left off? Patience. The word came blazing into her thoughts like a runaway train.

She would need patience for herself as well as Micah in the days to come. Patience to try and understand her own thoughts, some of which seemed to change with the weather, as well as patience for Micah and the annoying problems his profession presented.

Back in her room, Blythe showered and dressed for dinner. Earlier, she'd thought about having a sandwich by the pool and then going for a swim afterward, but the darkening clouds and now the steady sound of rain had wiped out that idea. That left Renaldo, she thought mischievously. Though there were two or three other dining rooms and a lounge, Blythe knew she couldn't resist harassing the unbending headwaiter in the Crystal Room.

Her entrance into the elegant setting some thirty minutes later had Blythe searching the dining room for Renaldo. Unfortunately, just as their gazes locked and she saw his nose quiver with dislike, Blythe found Stephen by her side.

"Great," he told her. "Micah said you might be eating alone." He offered her his elbow, and there was a cheeky grin on his face. "Will madame do me the honor of joining me for dinner?" he asked in a startling British accent.

Blythe stared hard at him.

"Something wrong?" he demanded.

"I'm not sure," Blythe murmured as she continued her examination. "I'm trying to see where the skin comes together."

Stephen frowned as he looked critically at the sleeve of his dark suit and even the legs of his trousers. "What the hell are you talking about?"

"That British accent was so beautiful and so unexpected from someone who usually doesn't give a damn, I'm convinced the Stephen Caine I know was skinned and his thick hide stretched over some other innocent person."

"Cute, real cute," he muttered. "If you don't promise to do better, I'll leave you in the loving hands of Renaldo. Speaking of Renaldo"—Stephen considered Blythe for a moment—"can you explain why either of us comes here to eat? We can't stand the man, and the food in the other dining rooms is just as good. Care to elaborate?"

"I could, but it wouldn't make either of us look too good. Get my drift?"

" 'Fraid so. What about us going to a little place I know about twelve miles down the coast? There's no music other than a jukebox, and from the outside it looks like a dump. But it's clean, and the food is heavenly."

"Do you think we should after last night?" Blythe looked a bit apprehensive.

"Ahh," he smirked. "This place is different. The only alcoholic beverage they sell is beer."

"Then that means I won't be having a drink before dinner. I hate beer."

The food was just as good as Stephen had predicted, Blythe remarked some time later as she sat back contentedly. "I'll have to remember this place. My aunts adore seafood."

"When are they due back?" Stephen asked.

"Tomorrow. They've wanted to go on a cruise for ages. When Micah said he could get them included on this three-day jaunt, they were delighted."

"I'm looking forward to seeing them. I remember them as being characters."

"Oh, they are, believe me. They're also willing to try almost anything, and are constantly on the go. You've never lived until you've gone shopping with my aunts."

"Bad, huh?"

"Unbelievable. It's as though they're afraid of hurting each shopowner's feelings if they don't stop in at every store. They try on enormous numbers of dresses, blouses, slacks—everything."

"Yet I see a gleam in your eyes when you speak of them. You care for them very much, don't you?"

"Yes"—Blythe nodded—"I do. They're my family. But what about you and Micah, Stephen? I can't remember him ever mentioning anybody but you. Weren't there any other relatives who could have stepped in and helped you?"

"There was an uncle, but Micah knew him better than I did and was convinced that if we went to work for him, he'd treat us like slaves. He decided that if that was to be the case, then he'd become a slave for himself. He did, and"—Stephen gestured with one hand—"you know the rest."

"You and Micah are very close, aren't you?"

"Yes. I suppose you could compare us to you and your aunts. We're alone, yet we're happy because we have each other. In the literal sense, of course. I think we both want families, but so far," he shrugged. "We haven't settled down. I think that's what Micah wants with you, Blythe."

"Do you really?"

"I certainly do. If not, why would he have

stayed single all this time, especially after he'd heard you had married? And then later, when he heard about your divorce, he was like someone with a new lease on life. You women get a hold on a poor man, and you keep it until the grave."

"Thanks heaps," Blythe remarked, her mouth bracketed with disgust. "You make us sound like leeches."

"Some of your fair sex are, honey." Stephen nodded as he stared into the foamy bottom of his beer mug. "Some of you are. Especially the ones who are so damn stubborn they won't listen to reason."

"Of course," Blythe said faintly. Without being told, she knew that something had triggered a responsive chord in Stephen, and he was remembering another place and time and another face sitting across from him. She made a mental note to ask Micah about it. Perhaps some sort of disappointment in love would account for his devil-may-care attitude and—at times—his cynical approach toward life. She glanced down at her watch and gave a faint gasp when she saw the time. "It's almost ten o'clock. I really think we should be getting on our way. Micah said he'd try to get through with his meeting as early as possible."

"And I bet he'll be delighted to get away. He's trying to decide what to do about a man who's been with him for nearly fifteen years and has been caught with his hand in the till."

"Oh, dear."

Conversation was kept to a minimum as the check was paid and as a wild dash was made through the rain for the car. After brushing the moisture from her skirt and running smoothing fingers through her hair, Blythe leaned back in her seat. "Tell me more about this man Micah is meeting with this evening."

"Oh, he's not actually seeing John this evening," Stephen told her. "That comes later in the week when Micah flies to Miami. It's the accountants that are at the hotel. They're trying to figure out how bad the corporation has been had. Seems ol' John had a really neat scheme going. Being a manager, he had access to every phase of the business. Consequently, when the hotel he was managing needed ten dozen towels, he'd order twelve. Replacement of six new lamps automatically called for an order of eight. The list goes on and on, from the kitchen down to the landscaping."

"What on earth was he doing with his, er, booty?" an astonished Blythe asked.

"Why, my dear," Stephen grinned mockingly, "he was running his own small hotel and showing a very nice income."

"That fink."

"Among other things. Now it's up to Micah to decide whether to press charges and send the man to prison or fire him and leave him with his wife and children. Either way, it's not an easy decision."

"I'm sure it won't be," Blythe agreed, just as a great clap of thunder sounded and a jagged streak of lightning was flung across the sky. The rain increased in intensity, making it difficult to see much. "This is awful."

"I agree," Stephen grunted, his gaze glued to the road in front of him, his wide shoulders tensed. "If I knew the road better, I'd pull off until it slacked off. Unfortunately, I can't see well enough to distinguish a small ditch from a ravine, so we'll just have to limp on in. Scared?"

"Terrified," Blythe confessed. "I've always been frightened of storms."

By the time they'd crawled across the causeway, the water on some parts of the island was ankle deep. The entrance to the hotel was jammed with stalled vehicles. Stephen gave a muttered curse, then continued on around toward the back. It was some distance from the main building, but the heavy rain made it impossible to get closer. "My bungalow is a lot closer than the hotel. We'll park here and make a run for it. Okay?"

"Yes," Blythe said loudly, not certain she wanted to leave the safety of the car but too afraid to stay by herself. She waited for Stephen's nod, then opened her door at the same moment he opened his. He caught her hand at the front of the car and pulled her along with him to the square building nestled in a grove of waving palm trees. The overhang along the front of the structure afforded them a measure of protection while Stephen unlocked the door.

They tumbled into the attractive front room of the bungalow like two shots out of a cannon.

"It's like the arctic in here," Blythe cried out, her hands clasping her upper arms. "Turn something off—quick."

"That's because you're wet, toots," Stephen chuckled, but he didn't offer the slightest protest as he went into the hall and adjusted the thermostat. He came back into the room and looked thoughtfully at his soggy guest. "Since it looks as though you're going to be here for a while, why don't you slip into my robe while I throw your clothes into the dryer?"

"That's the best idea I've heard all evening. Point me toward the robe and give me five minutes."

"Down the hall and to your right," he instructed her. "You'll find a terrycloth robe hanging on the back of the bathroom door."

Several minutes later, Blythe tied the belt of the robe as tight as she could and rolled the sleeves back at least three cuffs. Stephen and Micah must have descended from a line of giants, she thought amusedly. She'd never known such large, tall men.

She picked up her wet clothes, glanced around the bathroom to see that she hadn't left anything out of place, and then walked into the adjoining bedroom. She was halfway across the very masculine but pleasantly decorated room when something out of the corner of her eye caught her attention. She stopped and turned; her gaze went to a photograph of a lovely woman on the walnut chest. Blythe walked slowly over and stared at the smiling face, which looked as if it were about to speak to her.

The woman had the most remarkable eyes Blythe had ever seen. They were large and blue, fringed with thick sooty lashes and expressing pure devilment. Blythe had often heard the expression *heart-shaped face*, but this was the first time she'd really seen one. The remainder of the face was rather ordinary, she thought, if one considered a small, straight nose and a wide smiling mouth with perfect teeth ordinary.

"You were so quiet, I thought you'd gotten lost." Stephen spoke directly behind Blythe.

She jumped, her face turning apple red at being caught nosing around. "I—I'm sorry," she stammered, "but she's one of the most beautiful women I've ever seen. Is she a friend of yours?"

"Friend?" he repeated, his blue-gray eyes turning warm and cold in rapid succession as he stared at the photograph. He'd changed into a pair of faded jeans, leaving off a shirt and shoes. "I seriously doubt she's my friend."

Blythe placed her hand on his arm. "I'm sorry, Stephen. I didn't mean to pry."

"Don't worry about it, toots, I know you didn't." He threw a friendly arm across her shoulders, then leaned down and dropped an awkward kiss on her cheek. "Someday, when we've got a lot of time on our hands, I'll tell you about Val. In the meantime, let's go get something to drink that'll put a little fire in our veins."

"Looks to me like you've got about all the fire you can handle now."

Blythe whirled around. The sight of Micah standing in the doorway of the bedroom left her stunned. There didn't appear to be a dry thread on him, and his face was a mask of absolute fury.

"Micah. We didn't expect anyone to be out in this weather."

Stephen simply looked at Blythe and shook his head while Micah exploded with an accusing, "Apparently not."

"There's nothing going here, Micah, but two people getting in out of the rain and changing clothes. In separate rooms, I might add," Stephen said decisively. "The entrance to the hotel was blocked and we didn't want to swim to the lobby. I'm going to have some brandy. You're both welcome to join me if you care to."

Once Stephen had gone, Blythe continued to stare at Micah. He couldn't be thinking she was involved with his own brother, could he?

"Micah, would you mind telling me exactly why you're looking so furious?"

"I'm not exactly pleased about finding my woman in my brother's arms," he snapped.

"First of all, I am not your woman," Blythe said firmly. "And second, I was not in Stephen's arms. He was explaining something awkward, and the peck on the cheek was nothing more than time for him to regain his composure."

"At this point, I don't give a flaming damn whether or not my brother ever regains his composure," Micah lashed out at her. "I don't like seeing you in another man's arms. And just to set the record straight, you *are* my woman. Now, tomorrow—forever."

Blythe stared disbelievingly at him. "Go to hell!" She turned on her heel and started to rush past him.

"Oh, no, you don't," Micah said coldly as he whipped one long arm out and around her waist before she could blink an eye. He pulled her around to face him, holding her so close to him their bodies were touching. "I let you storm out of a room one time and it damn near destroyed us both. This time we'll leave together."

"I'm not going anyplace with you as long as you think I'm—I'm fooling around with Stephen," Blythe stormed at him.

"Does it bother you to think that I might not trust you, Blythe?"

"Of course it does," she countered.

"Don't you think that a certain amount of trust comes, or should come, with love?"

"This isn't a lesson in trust and fidelity, Micah," she said angrily. "What you've just said is true, but that doesn't excuse your behavior. This evening or last night."

"Do you believe I love you, Blythe?" he surprised her by asking.

"Yes," she answered in a subdued voice. What kind of game was he playing? she wondered. Love was a world apart from the hard anger emanating from him at the moment.

"Do you love me?"

"Yes."

"Does it hurt you to think I don't trust you?"

"Of course. If you really loved me, there would be no way . . ." her voice trailed off, her expression wary and at the same time there was the beginning of a different emotion, one that turned her from confusion to enlightenment. "You did this deliberately, didn't you?" she whispered.

Micah lifted one large hand to her face and pushed back the damp curls from her forehead. "Don't you ever believe it, honey. I'm not that much of a masochist. Call it Kismet—whatever. The facts remain the same. You were appalled that I could possibly think you guilty of being involved with Stephen, or any other man for that matter, weren't you?"

"Yes. And now I can see how you must have felt when I made that terrible mistake. So." Blythe smiled at him. "I'm sorry, I apologize, and all that. What about you?"

Micah tried for the injured look. "I don't know," he demurred. "You made me wait months and months. I deserve a small moment of revenge just for the hell of it."

"Ah." Blythe grinned at him, feeling suddenly as if the weight of the world had been lifted off her shoulders. "But what I did was completely innocent, and I was—and still am—considerably younger than you."

Micah gaped in mock surprise. "What the hell has age got to do with anything?"

"You're older, more mature. You've had more experience in life, so you should have known how to handle something as innocent as the blonde in your suite. And in the future, sweetheart," she purred as she raised her arms and encircled his neck, "in the event you walk into your bedroom and find a nude woman, a fully clothed woman, or even a totally blind woman, you'd better get the hell out of there and pray she doesn't follow you. Understand?"

"Completely." Micah smiled. He caught her close and covered her lips with his, his tongue seeking out hers and engaging it in a wild and exciting challenge. He raised his head, his breathing rough and ragged. "Something tells me I'm going to be indebted to my brother for a long time."

"Truer words were never spoken," Stephen sang out from behind them. "I've been clearing my throat for at least five minutes, but you two didn't hear me. I especially liked the part, Micah, where you're supposed to watch out for odd women in your bedroom. I'll be happy to do a room check for you anytime."

"You are a tactless twerp," Blythe said to him. "You are a complete toad for eavesdropping."

"I know, but it's so much fun. You should try it some time. By the way, your clothes aren't dry yet. And since it's getting late, would the two of you mind removing yourselves from my bedroom? I'm sleepy."

"You really expect us to go out in this storm?" Blythe asked, shocked.

"No. Only as far as the sitting room. When the storm lets up, I expect you to vamoose. I haven't the slightest desire to find you cuddled up on my sofa in the morning. It's bad for my hormones."

"Tell your hormones to take a hike." Micah dismissed his brother's remark without a care. "We may or may not spend the night—it depends entirely on the weather."

Stephen shrugged indifferently and walked into the bathroom and slammed the door, which almost drowned out the sound of his off-key whistling. Micah caught Blythe up in his arms and strode into the sitting room and over to the sofa before setting her on her feet. They sank into the overstuffed cushions, hungry for the taste and touch of each other.

"If this rain doesn't stop pretty soon," Micah groaned, "I'm afraid my brother is going to have to take medication for his hormones." He pushed himself up on his elbows and looked down at her, his hands idly twisting in and out of her hair. "Stephen left a note tonight, telling me where you had gone. But even still, I didn't like it."

"I'm sorry." Blythe turned her face and pressed her lips against a hand. "I really didn't think you'd mind. And I don't think you do," she said after a moment. "It's the newness of it, isn't it? After all the hurts and heartaches, you can't believe it's really happening, can you?"

"Yes to the first question and no to the last one," he muttered. "I suppose I'll lighten up with time." He shifted his position so that his large body was directly on top of hers. The weight of him almost buried her in the cushions. "This is cruel and inhuman torture," he breathed against her ear. "How do you feel about taking strolls at night?"

"I love walking," Blythe said honestly, "night or day."

Almost before the words were out of her mouth, Micah was standing beside the sofa, pulling her to her feet. "I do love a woman of decision." He flashed her a big smile, his teeth showing white against the darkness of his skin in the dimly lit room. Blythe felt one arm slip beneath her knees and the other behind her upper back with singlemindedness reminiscent of a bulldozer.

"Need some help, Micah, old buddy?" Stephen asked.

Micah whirled around, almost banging Blythe's head against the wall in the process. "You have the damnedest habit of creeping up on people. But since you're here, you can open the door for me."

Stephen willingly obliged, and as Blythe's laughing gaze collided with his cynical one, he lifted his brandy in a toast. But it wasn't the laughing faces of Micah and Blythe that he saw in that precise moment; it was rather the heart-shaped face that refused to die. He gazed up through the rain toward the heavens, his lips drawn back in an almost painful expression. Slowly he raised the glass again. "To you, Val, wherever you are."

CHAPTER SEVENTEEN

"He was a very nice man, dear," Amanda told Blythe, "in spite of what Carrie says about him. Of course, you do know what they say about nice people."

"Er, no. What do they say about them?"

"Boring," Carrie chimed in, receiving a stiff glare from her sister. "Oh, I'm sure he was a veritable saint, but the man was a dead bore. I tried to interest you in that lively Mr. St. John." She turned to Blythe. "Now there was a man."

"If he was such a catch, then why were you so interested in giving him to me?" Amanda wanted to know.

"Because he has horses, and you've always liked horses."

"I do, but not to the exclusion of everything else."

"On a scale of one to ten, would you say the cruise was a success?" Blythe asked. For the better part of nearly two hours she'd been entertained by her aunts. The stories were wild, and she'd almost split her sides laughing.

"It was nice for a few days," Carrie mused. "But I don't think I'd want to take an indefinite cruise. What about you, Amanda?"

"I feel the same. After a day or two, I found myself wanting to see some grass—feel some earth between my fingertips. But enough about us." She smiled. "Tell us what's been happening here. I understand Stephen is back. And how is Micah? Are the two of you getting along any better?"

"Stephen is back. The only change I can see in him is that he's more cynical. Micah is fine —from what I see of him. He's had a number of meetings since you've been away. I've done a bit of sightseeing, worked on my tan, and have been generally lazy. Having to get back into a solid routine is going to be absolute murder." Blythe chuckled.

"Oh, by the way," she added, "I did learn

something about the gentleman who had the unfortunate accident while waiting to see the condos."

Both Carrie and Amanda leaned forward, their expressions quite serious.

"What did you learn, dear?" Amanda asked.

"His name was Allen Johnson, and he was an accountant for a large corporation that makes some kind of valve for the government. At any rate, it's been learned that this corporation had been steadily bilking Uncle Sam out of millions through overcharging for the past few years. Mr. Johnson was head of accounting for the corporation and had decided to cooperate with the authorities. He was to have testified before a Senate committee next week."

"How awful!" Carrie murmured. "He seemed like such a nice man when we were talking about birds."

"Don't be such a ninny, Carrie," Amanda snapped. "Whether or not the man was a thief doesn't mean he'd lost all his senses of appreciation. I'm sure he still enjoyed eating, sex, and a number of things."

"And just what would you know about the

likes and dislikes of a thief?" Carrie demanded.

"I've read several books on the subject."

"Ha! Mystery novels aren't exactly books on any subject."

"It's better than an empty head."

"Well, if that's—"

"Girls!" Blythe quickly intervened before a fight could develop. "Why don't we table the discussion of Mr. Johnson for the moment, okay?"

"From the rosy glow on your cheeks, I assume the cruise was a roaring success." Micah had suddenly materialized beside the table.

"Micah!" Both older women spoke his name enthusiastically and smiled.

"We were just telling Blythe that, though we enjoyed the cruise, we're rather pleased to be back on firm ground again," Amanda informed him. She indicated the chair across from her. "Won't you join us?"

"Certainly." But before he sat down, he astonished them by walking around the table and dropping a warm kiss on Blythe's lips. One large hand caressed her shoulder, then slid down to hold her hand even as he sat down.

Amanda and Carrie exchanged glances. "I

must say, dear. Holding hands is a vast improvement over the arguing you two were doing with each other when we left," Carrie beamed.

Suddenly, a flash of pain fluttered across her face. She turned to Amanda. "Why on earth did you kick me?"

"Because you never know when to keep your mouth shut, that's why," Amanda snapped.

Micah's hand tightened on Blythe's, and they exchanged resigned looks as the battle began again. He leaned toward Blythe. "They seemed so peaceful when I walked up. What happened?"

"The reason they were so peaceful," Blythe sighed, "is because I'd just intervened so that your other guests wouldn't be subjected to a brawl between two senior citizens. As to what brought on this latest feud, I'm beginning to think they're simply unwinding. They've been cooped up together for three days. Need I say more?"

"No." Micah looked skeptically at Carrie and Amanda, wondering if they weren't on the verge of actually hitting each other. "But I don't envy you your role as peacemaker. At the moment, I suggest you do something before they kill each other. I never knew those sweet old ladies could be so vicious."

"That's because they like you. They're always on their best behavior when you're around," Blythe said resignedly. "I'm going to take Aunt Amanda to the Hartley Room, where they're playing bridge. Why don't you come up with something equally brilliant for Aunt Carrie?" she asked sweetly.

"Only if you promise to meet me at my place in thirty minutes," Micah said huskily, his eyes devouring her.

"Keep on looking at me like that, and I won't care if my aunts wreck this joint," she said dreamily.

Actually, it was almost forty minutes before Blythe was able to leave Amanda. She was ready to tear out her hair as she rode the elevator to the top floor, where Micah's apartment was located.

He must have had some sixth sense about when she'd arrive, because the moment the elevator whirred to a halt and the door slid open, Blythe stepped into his waiting arms.

"Now I'll think that every time I get off an elevator, I'm supposed to step into the arms of a handsome man," she murmured teasingly as her lips took playful nips at his stubborn chin.

"I doubt that."

"Don't become complacent, Mr. Caine," she said warningly. "No woman likes to be taken for granted."

"Oh, I'm not about to be guilty of that, sweetheart." He smiled. "I'll simply send one of your aunts along with you. Any poor bastard dumb enough to flirt with you with one or both of them present has my deepest sympathy."

"That's cruel." She leaned back against his arms and stared thoughtfully at him. "What's on your mind, buster?"

"You," Micah replied without batting an eye, "lying naked on my bed, waiting for me."

"For the life of me, I don't know why I bothered asking. That's all you think about." She sought a stern tone but failed miserably.

"Complaining already?"

"Never. Unfortunately, this morning, with my aunts around, I'm afraid your fantasy will have to be put on hold."

"I'll survive—maybe. In the meantime, come with me. I've got something to show you."

Blythe allowed her hand to be swallowed by his larger one, and she followed him into his apartment. "Wait here," Micah told her once they were in the sitting room.

In seconds he was back holding a tiny black box in his hand. He walked over and stood in front of Blythe. "I had this designed for you when I heard you'd divorced Talbot." He opened the velvet box, and Blythe gasped in astonishment at the beauty of the old-fashioned setting and the large pear-shaped diamond.

"It's beautiful," she whispered, awed that he could still have loved her even back then when she was positive she hated him. "Did you forget that I already have an engagement ring from you?"

He grinned rakishly. "How could I? You tried hard enough to give it back to me. But I want you to have this ring. Humor me on this, okay?"

"Okay," she murmured, then stood on tiptoe and kissed him. "It's really not necessary, though. I'd have been just as happy with my first one," she persisted.

"That ring belongs to a time in the past, Blythe." There was a hint of steel in his voice, and she smiled.

"Looking for a fight, Mr. Caine?"

Immediately the glint of anger became a

smoldering flame of passion. "You know exactly how to play me, don't you?" He wasn't touching her at all, but Blythe could feel the warmth and closeness of him like a caress. He caught her left hand then and slipped the ring into place. "That makes you mine now, sweetheart, in body and spirit." He raised her hand to his lips and pressed them against her finger and the ring. "I've sealed it—you can never take it off."

"I love you, Micah Caine," she whispered. There was a vulnerable luster of tears in her eyes as she witnessed his love for her. He'd remained steady in his feelings for her even when she was determined to cast him out of her life forever. Blythe wasn't sure she deserved this kind of love and said so.

"Don't," Micah placed the tips of his fingers against her lips. "If I don't criticize you, then don't you dare. You were in love for the first time, and I shattered your illusion. Now you're a woman. I feel very fortunate—I've known and loved you as a young girl, and I now know and love you as a woman."

"I want you to make love to me."

"I will, sweetheart, as soon as we can."

"No," Blythe told him. She stepped back and began unbuttoning the silk blouse she was wearing. "I want you to make love to me right now."

"But I thought you said—" Micah began, only to close his mouth as a smile slipped into place. "Being married to you, Blythe Donaldson, is going to be fantastic."

"Of course, Micah," she agreed, with invitation in her eyes as piece after piece of her clothing fell to the floor. In an incredibly short time she was naked. The pink tips of her breasts unconsciously beckoned him like tiny jewels.

His eyes slipped down the slim length of her, and his heart almost stopped beating. She was his. That one thought kept repeating itself in his head. She was his.

When his clothes were scattered with hers, Micah bent down and scooped her up in his arms and carried her to the bedroom. As he laid her onto the bed, his lips dropped to one nipple and cradled it with his lips. Blythe's short gasp of pleasure was like music to his ears, sending him further along her body, tasting and licking until Blythe was crying out with pleasure.

When he took her it was swift, plunging them both into a world where sight and sound disappeared and only touching and feeling were recognizable.

"This is incredible." Blythe stared in astonishment at the tall, slim man sitting next to her, and then at Micah, who was leaning against the edge of his massive desk. Two days had passed since she'd accepted Micah's ring, two days in which she'd been unbelievably happy. Now, she told herself, to suddenly be hit with something like this was something of a shock.

"Don't worry, Ms. Donaldson," Tom Gentry told her. "Your aunts are in no danger at all. From the report the investigating officers made, they were nothing more than innocent bystanders. They didn't even recognize the make of the vehicle."

"That's true." Blythe nodded, her face a study of apprehension. All of a sudden she looked up at Micah. "Did you tell Mr. Gentry about my aunts' suite being broken into?"

"When was this?" Tom quickly asked.

Micah related the incident, adding that he'd kept in touch with the local authorities, but they hadn't been able to come up with anything.

"Probably a coincidence since there have

been no other attempts. I'm sure that by now they've dismissed your aunts as not having the microfilm. Johnson was a stranger to them, and now that they've searched the ladies' suite, I'm sure they'll be left alone."

"Exactly what was on this microfilm you're searching for?" Micah asked.

"We suggested Mr. Johnson put all his information on tape, in the event something like this happened. Apparently, we have a departmental informant who passed on this information to certain members of the corporation. We know for a fact that Allen Johnson was to take the microfilm to a safety deposit box on the day he was murdered. Since he never showed up at the bank, we can only assume he hid the microfilm somewhere. The problem is, where? As I've said, I really don't think your aunts are in any kind of danger, Ms. Donaldson. But just to be on the safe side, you should keep a close eye on them. With your fiancé's staff, I'm sure that won't be much of a problem. Mr. Caine has my number if you need me."

Later during the same day, Tom Gentry questioned Amanda and Carrie at length. It could have been a harrowing experience for the two older women, but Tom was quite gentle with them, and they soon fell in with being interrogated so enthusiastically, they were disappointed when he had to leave.

Blythe was worried that something might happen to her aunts, but during the nights she spent in Micah's arms, he reassured her with his love and with every power at his disposal.

The days slipped by quickly until there were only three left. Tentative plans were made for Micah to follow them back to Mobile; Stephen would come a day or so before the wedding, the date of which was to be as soon as possible. Micah had also informed his bride-to-be that from that moment on, Stephen would be assuming more responsibility within the corporation, which would give Micah more time to be with his wife.

"I refuse to give you time to change your mind," Micah teased, but Blythe had read the insecurity in his voice. Consequently, she hadn't argued. Amanda and Carrie were thrown into a complete tailspin by the shortness of time given them to prepare for the wedding. Fortunately, the occasion caused them to call a truce. They spent the greater part of each day making lists of every conceivable nature. Either Micah, Stephen, or some member of the security staff was always close by.

Saturday dawned cloudy and dismal. Carrie wasn't feeling well and decided to sleep in, and Amanda had plans to go into town shopping with several other women whom she and Carrie had met on the cruise.

Blythe wasn't sure her aunt should go, but when she talked to Micah about it, he didn't see any problem. "She'll be in a crowd. Besides, I agree with Tom Gentry. It's been long enough now for them to have done something if they suspected Amanda or Carrie. Just caution Amanda not to go off anywhere on her own while she's away from the hotel."

During the morning Blythe looked in on Carrie, saw that she had plenty of orange juice and magazines, and then went for a walk along the beach. She finally decided to pay a visit to Micah in his office. Just as she entered the reception area, one of the two secretaries that worked for him looked up and saw Blythe. She quickly picked up the receiver and spoke into it, then hastly replaced it and rushed over to Blythe.

"Ms. Donaldson, we've been looking everywhere for you. Mr. Caine wants to see you at once."

"Oh, dear," Blythe said with a smile. "That has ominous overtones."

The minute she saw Micah, she knew something terrible had happened. "What's wrong?" Her words were barely audible.

"It's Amanda," Micah said quietly. He came around the desk and caught Blythe by the upper arms. "She's doing fine, but she was mugged."

"Mugged?" Blythe cried. "Who on earth would mug a woman in her seventies?"

"It's done every day, honey. Another lady in the group received some bruises when she tried to come to Amanda's aid. Fortunately, both women will be fine. We have to go down to the hospital to see her and to fill out the forms. We've also got to go by police headquarters and get her purse. Only she or a member of her family can claim it."

"Of course," Blythe murmured rather dazedly. She leaned against Micah, drawing strength from his vitality. Carrie was under the weather with the sniffles, and poor Amanda had been mugged. She closed her eyes and took a deep, steadying breath, then followed Micah to his car.

Aside from the purplish bruise on the right

278

side of her face, Amanda was fine. "Don't worry," she chided as she hugged Blythe to her. "I'm fine. I'm mostly mad as hell."

"That's the spirit." Micah chuckled. He dropped a quick kiss on Amanda's lined cheek and straightened. "We wouldn't let Carrie get out in this weather because of her cold, so you'd better call her soon. She's pretty upset. Stephen is with her."

"Poor dear, I'll do that. You know, Carrie isn't strong. I have to look after her."

After staying with Amanda until she dropped off to sleep and then having a chat with the doctor, who assured Blythe that her aunt was fine and would be released the next day, Blythe and Micah went to the police station to pick up Amanda's purse.

The desk sergeant handed Blythe a sturdy box, a comical grin on his face. "We normally put the purse and all into a large envelope. But we couldn't find an envelope your aunt's purse or contents would fit into. We'd appreciate you making sure everything is there. You'll find the inventory sheet on top there."

Micah thanked him, took the box and nodded toward a table near one wall. "While you're getting started on this, I think I'd better call and check on Carrie."

"Thanks, Micah." Blythe beamed up at him. "I really don't know what we would have done without you."

"Oh—you would have managed," he said quietly. "I'm just glad I was here. Hurry up with that, and I'll take you out to lunch."

"Will do." Blythe grinned, then sat back and watched him walk toward the bank of pay phones, loving every motion of his tall, strong body. She inhaled deeply, then began removing her aunt's belongings from the box, marking them off the inventory list and then placing them in Amanda's copious bag.

She was still hard at work when Micah returned. He sat down beside her and began poking through the box, a disbelieving expression on his face.

"I've never seen anything like this in my life," he murmured, awestruck. "Even if they'd gotten the purse, how in hell would they have ever found anything?"

"You're only saying that because you have no sense of organization," Blythe haughtily informed him.

"Organization, my behind," he scoffed. "That"—he pointed toward the box—"looks like one giant mess."

"It is." Blythe laughed. "But to Amanda,

every piece of paper, every rubber band, is vital. Except"—she eyed a foil-wrapped item she was holding between her thumb and forefinger—"one old cookie." She handed the crumbling tidbit to Micah. "Would you mind putting this out of its misery?"

Micah took it, his hand closing around the cookie. "Damn!" he exclaimed, opening his palm and probing it with his finger. "What the hell does your aunt put in her cookies, nails?"

"What?" Blythe smiled automatically, never looking up from what she was doing.

"I said—oh hell! No wonder Amanda was mugged." He held his hand beneath Blythe's nose, a tiny dark object resting in the middle of his palm. "Honey, I do believe we've just found out what Mr. Johnson did with his microfilm."

Greenleigh had never looked lovelier. Garlands of greenery and white satin bows festooned the graceful mahogany stair rail. Luxurious arrangements of early summer flowers added their glorious color to the stately dining and sitting rooms. Out on the lawn beneath a striped tent, a four-piece band was playing continuously and couples were dancing on the wooden platform laid out on the south lawn. Though the wedding was over, no one seemed in the mood to leave.

"Do you think the guests plan on living here?" Micah leaned down and spoke huskily against Blythe's ear. His hand was involved in the most delightful dalliance of running up and down her spine. "Does that bother you?" he whispered again.

"Yes," Blythe hissed at him. "It bothers me to the extent that if you don't stop, I'm going to attack you right here in Amanda's pansy bed."

"Good. I like to see you bothered. Now you know how it's been for me so many times in the past."

"You're a—how do you do, Mr. Somerville? So nice to see you and your sister. I don't believe you've met my husband?"

On and on it went until Blythe was certain her hand would drop off and her tongue was swelling. Finally, Micah took her hand and informed Carrie and Amanda they were leaving. Before Blythe had time to turn around, or so it seemed, she found herself beside Micah in a dark blue Mercedes, picking birdseed out of her hair.

"I wanted rice," he grumbled, flipping his

earlobe and sending a piece of seed flying. "What the hell kind of send-off is it having birdseed flung at you?"

Blythe smiled at his petulant tone. "Darling, birds eat the rice, and it can kill them. That's why we used birdseed. Doesn't it make you feel better knowing you're helping save our little feathered friends?" she teased.

"Not particularly," he stubbornly maintained. "My wedding day was ruined because I didn't get my rice."

"Don't pout," Blythe said as she dropped her head back against the seat. "Tomorrow I'll get you a fifty-pound bag of the stuff."

Late that evening, as Blythe stood before the window in the suite she was sharing with her husband and looked out at the sea, she closed her eyes against the prickling sensation of tears. She was so happy.

Suddenly she tipped her head to one side. Was that Micah? She listened. It was Micah, and he sounded as if he were in pain. She spun around and ran toward the bedroom door. Her hand automatically reached for the knob. But when she pushed against the door, it seemed to be stuck.

"Micah? Micah, are you all right?"

Without warning, the door opened. Blythe had taken only one step inside the bedroom when it felt and looked as if fifty pounds of rice were falling on her head.

"Micah!" she yelled. "Where are you, you worthless—" She walked blindly forward, shaking her head and brushing rice off herself. "Come out you coward, it will only hurt when I break one of your legs. By the time I get to the second one, you won't even know it."

One minute she was standing in the middle of the room with rice all over her, and the next thing she knew, she was picked up in a pair of strong arms and pressed against a broad chest.

"Threatening me already, huh?" Her husband grinned down at her.

"You're incorrigible."

"I know, but I love you." His eyes were smoldering with desire. "I'm hungry. Make love to me, Blythe Caine."

She did. But it wasn't until the early hours of the morning that his hunger was assuaged and the last fear of losing her was laid to rest. Micah Caine held his sleeping wife in his arms and looked upward in simple thanks.

Now you can reserve June's
Candlelights
before they're published!

- ♥ You'll have copies set aside for *you* the instant they come off press.
- ♥ You'll save yourself precious shopping time by arranging for *home delivery*.
- ♥ You'll feel proud and efficient about organizing a system that *guarantees* delivery.
- ♥ You'll avoid the disappointment of not finding *every* title you want and need.

ECSTASY SUPREMES $2.75 each
- ☐ 125 MOONLIGHT AND MAGIC, Melanie Catley 15822-2-96
- ☐ 126 A LOVE TO LAST FOREVER,
  Linda Randall Wisdom 15025-6-26
- ☐ 127 HANDFUL OF DREAMS, Heather Graham 13420-X-30
- ☐ 128 THIS NIGHT AND ALWAYS, Kit Daley 16402-8-19

ECSTASY ROMANCES $2.25 each
- ☐ 434 DARE TO LOVE AGAIN, Rose Marie Ferris 11698-8-21
- ☐ 435 THE THRILL OF HIS KISS, Marilyn Cunningham 18676-5-14
- ☐ 436 DAYS OF DESIRE, Saranne Dawson 11712-7-15
- ☐ 437 ESCAPE TO PARADISE, Jo Calloway 12365-8-47
- ☐ 438 A SECRET STIRRING, Terri Herrington 17639-5-38
- ☐ 439 TEARS OF LOVE, Anna Hudson 18634-X-49
- ☐ 440 AT HIS COMMAND, Helen Conrad 10351-7-13
- ☐ 441 KNOCKOUT, Joanne Bremer 14563-5-19

At your local bookstore or use this handy coupon for ordering:

DELL READERS SERVICE—DEPT. B1069A
P.O. BOX 1000, PINE BROOK, N.J. 07058

Please send me the above title(s). I am enclosing $_____ [please add 75¢ per copy to cover postage and handling]. Send check or money order—no cash or CODs. Please allow 3-4 weeks for shipment. CANADIAN ORDERS: please submit in U.S. dollars.

Ms Mrs Mr_____

Address_____

City State_____ Zip _____

A beautiful book
for the special people
who still believe in
love . . .

RICHARD BACH'S

The Bridge Across Forever

By the same
author who
created
<u>Jonathan
Livingston
Seagull,</u>
<u>Illusions,</u>
and <u>A Gift
of Wings.</u>

10826-8-44 $3.95

LAURA LONDON

Let her magical romances enchant you with their tenderness.

For glorious storytelling at its very best, get lost in these Regency romances.

___ A HEART TOO PROUD . .	13498-6	$2.95
___ THE BAD BARON'S DAUGHTER	10735-0	2.95
___ THE GYPSY HEIRESS	12960-5	2.95
___ LOVE'S A STAGE	15387-5	2.95
___ MOONLIGHT MIST	15464-4	2.95